RESHAPE WHILST DAMP

The Asham Awards' second collection of stories

Also published by Serpent's Tail

The Catch: The Asham Awards' first
collection of stories

RESHAPE
WHILST DAMP

Prize-winning stories by women

Edited by Carole Buchan

Library of Congress Catalog Card Number: 00–100500

A complete catalogue record for this book can
be obtained from the British Library on request

The right of the individual contributors to
be acknowledged as authors of their work has
been asserted by them in accordance with the
Copyright, Patents and Designs Act 1988

Copyright © 2000 of the individual contributions
remains with the authors

Compilation Copyright © 2000 Carole Buchan

First published in 2000
by Serpent's Tail,
4 Blackstock Mews, London N4 2BT

website: www.serpentstail.com

Set in Sabon by Intype London Ltd.
Printed in Great Britain by Mackays of Chatham plc

10 9 8 7 6 5 4 3 2 1

Contents

Foreword *Carole Buchan* vii
Downsizing *Vicky Grut* 1
Year Zero *Lynne Truss* 14
Anything You Can Do *Ruth Shabi* 23
Dogs of Athens *Elspeth Barker* 30
Guatemala Moon *Clare Bayley* 38
Exposure *Helen Cleary* 51
Friends *Barbara Trapido* 61
The Professional Wedding Attendee
  Aoi Matsushima 74
Deptford Girls *Kate Mosse* 84
The Iron Claw *Marion Mathieu* 95
Monsieur Mallarmé Changes Names
  Michèle Roberts 107
Skin Sins *Sarah Johnson* 116
Girls in their Loveliness *Ann Jolly* 131
The Lighthouse Keeper's Wife *Helen Dunmore* 144
The Mixing of Mendhi *Harkiran Dhindsa* 153
Reshape Whilst Damp *Ros Barber* 165
About the Authors 177

Foreword

When the first Asham Award was launched in 1996, nearly a thousand unknown women writers took part. The first anthology of winning stories, published a year later and entitled *The Catch*, demonstrated not only the rich cultural mix of our society today, but the huge range of largely untapped talent in the towns and villages across the United Kingdom.

The second Asham Award again attracted almost a thousand entries. This time, the brief was to 'kick-start the new millennium with writing which is different... extraordinary and ground-breaking'. We believe that this collection of stories does just that... and more. The judges were looking for writing to wake up... shake up... excite and galvanise as the century came of age. The range of subject, style and setting was enormous. And the judges had the unenviable task of choosing just ten for publication. Yet although the standard was high, the winners emerged almost immediately and the verdict was unanimous.

We believe that this collection of work encapsulates the finest traditions of short-story writing – a medium which is becoming increasingly popular in our rollercoaster world. But the short story is no easy way out for a writer. It demands great discipline and the ability to capture a mood, a moment, an emotion in just a few sentences.

The Asham Literary Endowment Trust seeks to give opportunities to new writers by publishing their work alongside those of established writers. We are delighted

Foreword

therefore that this anthology includes specially commissioned stories by Elspeth Barker, Helen Dunmore, Kate Mosse, Michèle Roberts, Barbara Trapido and Lynne Truss.

We are grateful to our judges – Kate Mosse, Lynne Truss and Pete Ayrton of Serpent's Tail – for their enthusiasm and good humour and to Serpent's Tail for supporting the Trust and its work. Special thanks also to Waterstone's, who have again sponsored the competition, and to Lewes District Council and East Sussex County Council, for sharing with us a belief in the future of women's writing.

Carole Buchan
Administrator, Asham Literary Endowment Trust
Lewes, East Sussex

Asham Awards 2000

First prize   Ann Jolly
Second prize   Ros Barber
Joint third prize   Clare Bayley and
                      Aoi Matsushima

Downsizing

Vicky Grut

When he was still Head of Department, back in the days when Policy and Evaluation still existed as a department, Martin used to like to hold forth on the future of work. 'In the knowledge-based economy, we will ask people to work "smarter" not "harder",' he would say, 'and until this old place catches on, it's heading for oblivion.' The words he forgot to mention, Julianne thought afterwards, were 'cheaper' and 'younger'.

After the Organisational Restructuring, perhaps because of the speed at which the security guards helped him out of the building, Martin left much of his library on management theory behind. Julianne offered to share it with Tom but he wasn't interested, so Julianne took the books home and read them in the evenings while her mother watched TV. Julianne found their language reassuring, uplifting even. In future, they said, organisations would disaggregate into a complex mix of profit centres, franchises, small firms and sub-contractors. Companies would retain a small core of permanent employees but most of those in work could expect to function as 'portfolio people', delivering services to a range of clients. Command and control management would be a thing of the past. She and Tom, Julianne discovered, had already arrived in 'computopia'. How lovely, she thought.

It was true that, in the new era, their work was far cleaner. Most of the information they needed could be obtained by e-mail and their reports were lodged in the same way. They did not have to waste time communicating with other members of their own department since there were none; and soon the names of other departments – 'payroll', 'press office', 'research and development' – ceased to conjure up a muddle of names and faces. They got a lot more done.

But it was lonely down in the basement. Sometimes Julianne would think about the old office on the fifth floor, and how she used to watch the sun turn the river pale as paper at the end of the day, the way the glass buildings seemed to burn. Where they were now, the only window faced a blind wall and the sun seldom found its way into the room. The silence was punctuated at intervals by urgent liquid thunderings from the men's room on the floor above them, and through the wall behind her desk she could hear the crunch and grind of the lifts.

'I reckon we should approach them with a project,' Tom said after six months or so, when they'd begun to feel relatively safe again. 'We should offer to do a post-Restructuring audit; a kind of economic health check of the whole organisation. Otherwise they'll just forget we exist.'

Julianne touched the acupressure point on her neck and considered him thoughtfully. He was a small, neat man several years younger than she was. He had broad hands with moonlike nails, big ears, tiny eyes and fine teeth. He wore his fox-brown hair in a neat brush cut and his solid coloured shirts (pumpkin, biscuit, slate), buttoned up to the top without a tie. He was good at his job, Julianne thought. He had a knack of skimming through pages and pages of data, then coming up with small but startling insights. She was not particularly interested in men – they were all much of a muchness, her mother said – but there was something very pleasant about Tom.

'You go and talk to them,' he said. 'You've read all those fancy books, haven't you? You've got the lingo.'

After the meeting, Julianne found herself running back along one of the endless corridors on the fourteenth floor, her feet clattering wildly on the parquet. She couldn't move nearly fast enough. At the first vacant office she came to, she went in and rang Tom's extension number.

'What's happened? What did they say? Where are you now?' Tom's voice sounded compressed, pared down to the essentials.

'I'm still up here on the fourteenth floor. Oh, I wish you could have seen their faces!' She slapped the flat of her hand against her thigh. 'If we play this right, we can have them eating out of our hands!'

'Is the meeting finished?'

'You can't see any of this, can you?' She stopped and looked around her. She could see the river again: today it was choppy and almost black. 'It's quite extraordinary from up here. I'm in an empty office, just looking out, and oh my . . .' Julianne laughed. She didn't feel like hanging up at all. She felt a kind of slow uncoiling of something in her veins.

She had always found it easier to talk on the phone. You didn't have to worry about arranging your body appropriately or how your face was behaving or where the other person's eyes were straying. You didn't have to worry about whether your breath smelled, or whether theirs did, or about any unwelcome invasions of your personal space. She settled herself on the empty desk. Her breathing slowed. She smiled, touched a hand to her neck again, and heard the rustle of her hair.

'What can you see?'

'There's a storm brewing,' she said. 'At the moment there's just the wind but the light is changing very fast and I think there's rain on the way. There are clouds coming in. Fat, purple clouds and all the time the wind is stirring up the sky. There's bits of paper and leaves and birds being blown backwards. Everything is whipping about in the air. Everything is inside out and all over the place.'

There was a silence.

'You know what I'd like to do now?'

Still this crowded quiet on the line. She could hear his surprise and unease and excitement all coiled up together in the tightness of the optic fibre. 'What . . .' he cleared his throat, 'what would you like to do?'

She laughed. 'I'd like to open the window and step right out into the middle of it all.'

'Don't do that,' he said quickly.

'I'm only talking,' she laughed. 'Stupid.'

When she got back to her desk she could feel him watching her but he said nothing about the phone call; nor did she. They started planning the audit project together as if nothing had happened. This must be what the books meant, thought Julianne, about manufacturing trust.

They designed and circulated detailed questionnaires to every department. They constructed a database and a statistical model, they broke the results of the questionnaire into inputs and outputs. It took them almost exactly a year. During that time, Tom and his wife increased the size of their mortgage and moved from a flat to a house; took package holidays in Greece and the Canary Islands; and talked vaguely about having a baby but agreed they weren't quite ready. Tom had twenty-five haircuts (all the same), and visited his dentist once for a minor filling. He turned twenty-seven on the day they completed the last of the data entries.

Julianne took no exotic holidays, preferring to spread her leave across a series of short visits to friends (since her mother didn't like her to be away for long), but she did think about moving. She was nearly thirty and she longed now for a place of her own. She got as far as contacting estate agents before her mother's angina flared up again. Julianne had ten haircuts during this time (changing the style twice), eight sessions in a flotation tank, twelve Chinese massages to release stress and three visits to an osteopath about a stabbing pain in her neck (her teeth were perfect). If these appointments fell during working hours, she would always ring the office.

After a while she began to ring on other days too. Not carelessly, by any means. She rationed herself. She'd make herself wait until she couldn't bear to wait any longer. Then she'd run back up to the empty room on the fourteenth floor. 'It's me,' she'd say. And Tom would reply, 'I was wondering when I was going to hear from you again,' as if she was another person entirely. She loved that. Five minutes later she'd be back behind her desk and they'd both behave as if nothing had passed between them.

The picture that emerged from their analysis of the questionnaires was clear. They could see that, even after the restructuring, whole overweight sub-sections and divisions remained hanging on the organisation like ticks on a dog, sucking up money and time. The animal must be shaved right back to the bone, then they would see it move, sleek and lean and full of hurt, going in for the kill.

'This is going to blow their socks off,' Tom would mutter to himself as he worked on his section of the report. But Julianne was less satisfied; she felt there was something missing. At home she was irritable and distant with her mother, only happy when she could retire to her room and read her management theory books. Work, said the books, should be reconceptualised as a pool that you moved to the centre of rather than a pyramid that you climbed. The aristocracy of the labour market would be the 'symbolic analysts' (consultants, planners, advertising executives).

Julianne began to have dreams at night where she saw herself walking down long corridors with jigsaw-like chunks of her body missing. Or she would be back on the fourteenth floor, and the head of personnel would say, 'We'll wait another minute or so for Ms Stack and then I'm afraid we'll have to start'; and it would come to Julianne in a horrifying flash that they couldn't see her because she had been disaggregated, atomised, deleted.

By day Julianne wrote and rewrote her section of the report, delaying the very last sentence for as long as she could. She thought of Martin's books: when you found yourself in a blind alley, they said, it was best to turn your back on the problem and do something entirely different: swim, climb a mountain, dive from a plane – then, nine times out of ten, the solution would come to you suddenly, easily, like an egg dropping into your hand. She'd switch off her computer, then, and run up to the fourteenth floor: 'It's me. Did you miss me?'

'Of course. Tell me what you see?'

'Today? Oh, today the river is the colour of . . .' Bananas, steam trains, the old Rover my Dad used to drive – she could sit up here and tell him anything and he would have to believe her. As she talked, she felt perfectly light and safe, and all her worries would be suspended by the limits of the line. But she knew also how tenuous it was, how easily it could be interrupted.

Tom tried calling once. He must have gone out to a payphone because she could hear the swish of traffic in the air around him. His voice sounded harsh and grating in her ear.

'I dream about you, you know,' he said. 'I dreamed about you last night.'

Panic rolled under Julianne's skin: all the way up her back and over the top of her head. She nearly threw down the receiver, but she made herself count to ten. From the floor above came the melancholy roar and hush of water in the pipes.

With great effort she kept her voice steady, 'You don't understand this, do you, Tom? You're trying to force the pace, hurry us along to the punchline. But what if there isn't one? Hmm?' There was one of those dense, struggling silences on the line. 'You have to stop thinking in terms of ladders and pyramids and getting to the point. Think of this as a pool. Enjoy the moment. Swim, Tom, stop trying to climb.' She could hear him drowning out there, wherever he was. 'I'm hanging up now, okay?'

Later she went up to central admin. support and got them each a tiny matt black plastic mobile phone by way of compensation. 'In case of an emergency,' she said. 'We should be able to contact one another.'

'What's your number?'

She saw how he couldn't quite meet her eye, how his pen trembled above the page of his address book. 'No need for that,' she said. 'I'll make the calls.'

'Oh,' he said. He set down his pen.

She slipped her mobile in her shoulder bag, slung over

one hip; he dropped his in the breast pocket of his jacket, watching her. She could see he still didn't get it.

'It has to be me calling or it doesn't work,' she said. 'I have to be in control.'

The next time Julianne stepped out of the lift on the fourteenth floor, she found everything swathed in dust sheets and the air heady with the smell of paint. Workmen in overalls were busy packing up for the day, stacking ladders and trestles against the walls, dumping rollers in tubs, sealing up big industrial containers of paint.

'What's going on?' she asked a man who stood wiping his hands on a paint-soaked rag. The smell of turps spread around him like an itch.

'Don't know, love,' he grinned. 'We've got a contract to redecorate the whole of this floor. Maybe they're renting it out? Who knows. They never tell us what they want it for.'

Julianne walked down the main corridor with offices peeling off on either side. She stopped at the door to the boardroom where she'd pitched their audit idea more than a year earlier. It was like all the rest now: clean, featureless, gleaming white. She could almost feel the next wave of occupants piling up behind her, impatient to move in and make their mark. What work would they do here? Management consultancy, political lobbying, PR – jobs that left no residue, jobs you didn't have to wash up after at the end of the day.

From the lifts she heard faint clangs and shouts, then silence as the last of the painters left the floor. She walked on to the little boxroom at the end of the corridor. There was a single hinged window, looking out on the roof of the next building a couple of feet away. Julianne opened the window, leaning out as far as she dared to catch a splintered glimpse of the street.

Sometimes she toyed with the idea of applying for a job in a smaller place where she could be near the countryside and breathe fresh air. Her mother would go all pale and trembling when she talked like that. 'You always were like your father,' she'd say. 'Go on then. Go on. Walk away and leave me like this. I managed once, I suppose I'll manage again.' But Julianne knew she would never do it. It wasn't just guilt; it was her love of the city itself. She liked the buzz, the anonymity, the competitive edge. If she put her mind to it, if they made a success of this report, there would be opportunities to move to a better job, something one or two ripples closer to the centre. She wouldn't really be satisfied with anything less now.

She reached into her little bag for the phone. 'Tom,' she said. 'Come up here a minute, would you? I want to try out something. The fourteenth floor. Hurry.'

They took two great, solid planks from one of the painters' trestle tables and in no time at all they had built a bridge from the window where they stood to the roof of the opposite building.

Tom grinned: 'Now what?'

'I want you to walk across.'

Tom's face turned chalky with surprise. He looked from her to the window and back. 'Why would I do that?'

'How long have we been working on this report, Tom?'

'A year.'

'A whole year we've been buried down in that airless, lightless undergound box of an office and you know what, Tom? We've gone stale. We've lost our focus.'

'What's that got to do with me going out on that plank?'

'Sometimes, when you're working really hard you go sort of blind, Tom. You lose your sense of perspective and you need to stop and walk away from whatever it is you're doing. Sometimes it helps to do something apparently pointless: hot air ballooning, abseiling. Take a few risks and suddenly you see things from a different angle. I swear, that's what the books say.'

Tom stared at her for a long moment. Then he reached into his jacket pocket for the little phone, clasping and unclasping it in the palm of his hand. 'I'll do it if I can make one call.'

Julianne felt her throat constrict, but nodded. It was a fair trade-off: one fear for another. He took off his jacket, then knelt and checked his shoe-laces, hitching up his trousers so that they wouldn't get creased. Over by the window he stepped onto an upturned paint container, grabbed the window frame and hauled himself up onto the ledge. He crouched there for a long while, one foot on the planks, the other foot curled over the firm lip of the sill, both hands gripping the window frame.

'Go on, Tom,' Julianne whispered, 'you can do it.'

He stood up, still holding onto the window frame but ducking his head out beyond it, keeping his knees still slightly bent. He edged his foot out a little way onto the planks, turning his body towards the open window. His shirt brushed the glass, his fingers clung and crawled along its metal ridge, his left foot slid further out onto the boards, till there was nothing but air beneath the wood. Slowly, slowly, still gripping the window frame with one arm, he pulled his body round till he faced the opposite building and his back was to Julianne. And she was struck suddenly by the frail physical fact of him.

This is Tom, she thought, a bundle of flesh and blood and brain, a mass of raw human potential: flexible; suggestible; young; cheap; perfect.

'Go on, Tom,' she whispered. He slid his right foot up to meet the left, his fingers came clasp-clasping to the end of the window and fixed on the right-angle, holding it like the knob of a cane. Julianne couldn't move, not even to suck breath into her lungs. She couldn't blink. She knew that if her eyes let him go, if she stopped concentrating even for a moment, everything would be lost. She was reduced to nothing but this moment, this place, this body in front of her. He muttered something but the wind carried it off. His left foot edged forward, then he let go of the window and edged out of its reach. This is what it's all about, she thought.

'You can do this, Tom.'

Suddenly he was crouching in the middle of the bridge. He wobbled, then righted himself. 'Oh Jesus!' he shouted. 'Oh help me God!' but he was laughing at the same time.

Julianne frowned. What was he doing? He lurched, then righted himself, all the while fumbling for something in his shirt pocket. Another off-centre swoop and both arms flew out on either side of him. She saw the mobile in his one hand. He brought his arms in again very slowly. After a moment the phone rang at her hip.

'Hello?'

She closed her eyes and imagined him out there, in the middle of nowhere: thin as a toothpick, air swirling round his ears. 'Tom,' she said, 'you're doing really well, but don't lose your focus. Keep looking over at the far side and try . . .'

He cut her short. 'This is my call, Julianne. I talk and you listen this time, okay?'

Julianne was silent.

'Okay?' he said again. He took a big breath. 'This time I am going to let it all out: all those things that crawl around in my brain night and day and drive me crazy. Sometimes I think that everything I'm not allowed to say to you is collecting up in a huge ball of mucous in my throat and that one day it's going to rise up and choke me right there at my desk. Sometimes I think... no, I'll start with the dreams, sometimes, Julianne, I... whooo!... Christ! What a *rush* this is. What a high...' he started laughing wildly. Julianne held the phone away from her ear. 'A shagging great fourteen-storey high!' he was yelling. 'What a feeling. What an incredible feeling!'

Julianne looked out at the little figure teetering in the dirty afternoon air. She spoke softly into the phone again. 'Tom. This is serious. You must calm down. Concentrate. Otherwise you'll fall.'

'I swear,' he yelled, 'I'll never be afraid of anything in my life again, Julianne. Oh baby, when I get back in there I won't need a phone to say things I want to say to you. No! Things are going to be different from now on, sweetheart. I am not going to put up with... Tell me something, did you try this stuff on Martin? Is that why they got rid of him? Or am I losing my sense of perspective? What the hell. What difference does it make. Let me tell you about my dreams. In my dream you're in this short green skirt and you're standing on a ladder just behind my desk and I know that if I turn my head...'

Julianne stopped listening at this point. She had a sudden flash of insight, just as the books said she would. She understood three things: (1) that Tom did not perform well under pressure; (2) that she was looking at an image of the future – that this was the way their children and their children's children would work: without nets or props, nerveless and weightless and up against the wire; and (3) that her next job would be in some kind of management capacity. It was remarkable the way these three things simply floated into her head: complete and finished.

'... and you're wearing this really thin shirt and... whoo...'

Julianne looked out of the window in time to see him lurch again. Both his arms flew out to right his balance, but this time the mobile phone kept going. Julianne followed its trajectory through the air: a high, sweet arc which was quite irresistible to the eye. Only when the phone peaked and began to plummet did Julianne look back at the bridge.

For a moment she didn't move. Then she lifted a hand to caress the acupressure point on her neck. 'Oh dear,' she murmured.

Year Zero

Lynne Truss

The Sunday morning Rupert's dear deceased mother turned up at our front door wearing a bewildered expression, I'll admit I wasn't the least surprised. Midway through an argument, Rupert was shouting about how I never respected his feelings, and I was yelling that of course I respected his feelings, in fact I rarely did anything else, and poor little Jumbly was wailing in his cot, when there was an inconvenient knock at the door. At first I put down the wok I'd been wielding, but then I grabbed it back. If it was the neighbours again, I might as well carry a bit of self-defence.

But it wasn't the neighbours. It was this extremely well-accoutred old woman with discreet liver spots, a Hermès scarf and a faraway look on her face. Her slingbacks were ivory suede and absolutely lovely.

'Mrs Upton,' I said, extending a hand for her to shake. I recognised her from Rupert's photograph albums. 'You don't know me, I'm Suzanne. What gorgeous shoes.'

'Mother?' exclaimed Rupert, as he hurried to join me. 'Mother?' It was more of a shriek than a question. 'Suzanne,' he demanded, turning to me, 'isn't this getting a little out of hand? My mother is dead, for heaven's sake!'

The old woman blinked and inspected her fingernails. She looked incredibly good for a dead person. Quite peachy. No sign whatever of putrefaction. Not even a cobweb draped across a vacant eye-socket. In one hand was a thick, dog-eared paperback, which she was clearly keen to get back to. 'Hello Rupert,' she sighed, matter-of-factly. Remembering his manners at last, her only son leaned forward and kissed her.

'I'm sorry, dear,' said Mother, still on the threshold. 'Am I being impossible?' She shrugged and indicated an array of immaculate pigskin luggage.

'Well, quite honestly, yes,' Rupert said. 'Given that we buried you eight years ago. Surely you remember? You fell in front of a miniature engine on the Romney, Hythe and Dymchurch Railway while absorbed in a Roald Dahl collection. We had the music from *Tales of the Unexpected* at the funeral.'

Mrs U patted his hand and then pulled the extendable handle of a neat cabin bag. 'Shlack, shlack' it said as it reached full length in her grip. She tilted the bag, kicked it neatly in the shins, and entered the hall.

'Well, I'm here now,' she said, matter-of-factly. 'Where do you want me to stay?'

I suppose I should mention at once that the house was pretty full at this stage. 'It's to do with the arguments,' I explained repeatedly to Rupert, but he wouldn't listen. It seemed pretty clear to me, though. I once heard a theory about relationships which said that you've only got one bucket, and if it's full up with unresolved stuff from previous people in your life, there's no room for any more. Why a bucket I don't remember. I've not seen myself in such an Addis-y light before. But I know the full-capacity, swish-swosh, cubic-litre feeling, all right. And the way most of us are going around with our buckets overflowing it's like something from 'The Sorcerer's Apprentice', if you ask me.

You see, Rupert and I had been together for two and a half years, which was a record for us both. We were bickering a fair bit and sometimes simply lost the plot. And my point is: it surely happens in most relationships? Once you've both been round the block a few times you're all too likely to accuse each other of the wrong stuff, using arguments still hanging around from previous lives. It's the downside of quick-turnover serial monogamy. I've been married twice; Rupert's had heaps of girls. We were completely committed to each other; I'm not saying that. It's just that if you asked either of us, I'm confident neither of us would have been able to tell you our current telephone number, let alone whether we got married this time round.

Anyway, I assumed there was a connection with the barneys – this summoning up of people we should have emptied from our buckets. Because it wasn't just Mother, you see. Brian, my terrible ex who never gave me any space – he was taking up the spare room, while Rupert's two previous live-ins, Allison (hopeless pianist; finished his sentences) and Julia (neurotic washer and checker), were resident in the walk-in wardrobe. Each had turned up while we were engaged in lively – if unfair – personal debate. My tutor from Oxford (exploited my need for approval) and half a dozen of Rupert's old Bryanston chums (expected too much commitment) helped swell the household; also a small dog called Martin I'd owned as a teenager (constant nameless reproach).

If it helps to explain, this was how it started.

'That's another thing,' Rupert said one day in annoyance. We were arguing, as I recall, about the mess in the living room, and I'm sure we could have sorted it out.

'Suzanne, you always—' Rupert stopped, speechless. 'You always, you always—'

'I always what?' I asked, shrugging.

'You finish my sentences!' he said. Well, I gasped at the injustice of the accusation. Not only do I never finish people's sentences, but I happened to know it was something Rupert particularly disliked, on account of his old girlfriend Allison.

'That's very unfair,' I said. At which point Allison came through the French doors, sat down at the piano, and ran a polished fingernail lightly down the keys before starting a halting, whoopsadaisy, third-time-lucky rendition of *Für Elise*.

'Who's that?' I asked. Rupert blinked wildly.

'Good God, it's—' he began.

'Allison, yes,' Allison supplied. She took off her shoes. Rupert and I exchanged glances.

'Sorry,' I said. 'It's just we weren't—um—'

'Expecting me. No.'

So Allison moved in and we tried not to think about it. After a few days we just locked the piano and hid the key. But then Brian's entrance took a similar class of biscuit, and – although Rupert at first refused to accept it – I began to realise we had a syndrome on our hands.

'You don't give me any space, Rupert!' I yelled one night. And the sash window went up right behind me and Brian climbed in, brushing snowflakes off his jacket. And I have to admit I shrieked. I wouldn't have minded so much, but we were upstairs at the time.

'Only me,' he said, and stood right beside me, his shoulder touching mine. I backed off a bit and, true to old form, he moved with me, to maintain the contact. And then he took my hand.

We all looked at each other. Rupert said, 'I don't quite—'

'Know what to make of it,' said Allison, entering.

The four of us looked at each other. Rupert, me, the sentence-finisher and the human leech. It was a situation.

'I'll make us some coffee,' I volunteered, at last. 'And no, you can't come with me,' I added, for Brian's benefit, when I realised he was intending to accompany me. Good grief, there never was such a clingy man in the whole world.

'I only wanted—' Brian began.

'To help,' said Allison.

I looked round and all three of them appeared to be pouting at me. It was intolerable.

'Look, you lot. Don't use all that big-eyed emotional blackmail stuff on me. You know I can't stand it.' Which I suppose must have been a bit unfair because the moment I said it, I heard a long forgotten 'Yap yap' in the middle distance.

A dog? Did we own a dog?

'Yap yap yap.' The dog was approaching at considerable speed. I could hear its claws on polished wood as it scampered in our direction.

'Martin?' I said. And the little dog Martin – dead these ten years – appeared from nowhere, skidding across the parquet until he came to rest at my feet.

I wish I could say it was fun having these old flames and deceased pets around, but it wasn't. Especially as you never knew who might turn up next, dead or alive; or indeed animal, vegetable or mineral. Talking of vegetables, Rupert's mother was the worst, because she really didn't give a jot for Rupert's feelings. He had been quite right. Her indifference to everybody in her emotional vicinity was so pronounced that I could quite understand why her only son fought a lifelong battle for attention, even when the source of his pathetic insecurity had long since fallen beneath the wheels of a novelty locomotive, and even when other people were actually quite happy to give him attention in the usual amounts.

'Never let them see you care,' she advised me one day, as I rushed to pick up a weeping Jumbly for a cuddle. 'It makes them expect it.' And with that priceless pearl of maternal wisdom delivered, she returned to her Anne Rice.

'Fancy a trip to the Bluebell Railway, Mother?' I asked brightly, through gritted teeth. 'You could bring your book.'

The thing is, what do you do when your marriage is suddenly invaded by your former loved ones, the people you thought you'd left behind? I wished I could ask advice from my own mother, but it was pointless. She had married in 1947 and remained with the same man for over fifty years. She was unfamiliar with the modern problem of serial relationships except as it affected her, when it came to birthdays and Christmas and such.

'So what shall I get Brian, I mean Alan, I mean Jeremy?' she would ask on the phone.

'Actually, it's Rupert now,' I would say.

'Oh yes. Rupert. Jeremy was the one who was ever so literal-minded and collected Barbie dolls, wasn't he?'

'That's right. At the last count he had two hundred and seven.'

'Two hundred and seven?' She appeared to be taking this in.

I always felt I should defend Jeremy, to prevent her from asking what I had seen in him. What was it this time? Oh yes: 'I think he helped me with my feminine side,' I said lamely.

'That's nice.' A pause. 'Do you see him any more?'

'No, never.'

'It's a funny world you live in, Suzanne.'

'Yes.' You don't know the half of it, I thought. Especially as Brian had just put his arm around my shoulder, and was digging his chin into my neck. Meanwhile Julia, in the kitchen, was switching the oven on and off and muttering to herself (she'd been doing it all day).

'I don't know how you keep track.'

'No.'

A pause, while I considered whether to explain that it would be only a matter of time before a big van delivered Jeremy and his enormous plastic harem to my house.

'Do you remember Martin?'

'I don't think so. Did he have a beard?'

'I mean Martin the dog. That Daddy bought for me.'

'Oh yes. I always felt a bit sorry for Martin. We weren't really good enough for him, were we?'

I looked down to where Martin was regarding me with tragic wet eyes, one paw raised. There was something in his expression that suggested he had always depended on the kindness of strangers.

'I know what you mean,' I said.

The obvious solution was to stop arguing, of course. But we'd tried that and it hadn't worked. We had even made a list of everyone in danger of turning up – Jeremy, for example – together with the left-over emotions we still carried around with us about these people.

'So Jeremy was very literal-minded?' said Rupert. 'Was there anything else you couldn't stand about him?'

'He was jealous and superficial and defensive. And he wouldn't put the loo seat down. But I think that's all.'

'Well, that's nothing like me,' said Rupert, somewhat smugly. 'So I don't think there's any danger you'll accuse me of any of that. The Barbie collection may yet be kept at bay.'

'Don't be so sure,' I said. 'I mean, look how we got some of the others. How much am I like Julia? The mad washer and checker? Yet we managed to conjure her up when you happened to mention in a rather argumentative tone that I always turned off the taps too tightly.'

'Well, you do.'

'No I don't. Not always.'

'Yes you do. Nine times out of ten.'

'That's not the point.'

'Yes it is.'

As his voice rose, my heart sank. Wasn't this how it always got started?

'Rupert, be careful!' I warned.

'Don't tell me to be careful!'

'I only said—well, you know what happens.'

'And that's my fault, is it?'

'Good God, why are you always so *defensive*?' I yelled. Which was when we both stopped aghast and looked at Jeremy's list.

'Yike,' I said, dancing on the spot. 'I take it back, I take it back, I take it back.'

The doorbell rang.

'I take it back, I take it back, I take it back,' I whined, pleadingly.

But it didn't do the slightest bit of good. Jeremy's collection of Barbies now numbers two hundred and forty-eight. You've got to admire the dedication, haven't you?

Rupert and I split up, in the end. It was jolly sad, considering we were desperately fond of each other, but it was also a relief since we had to admit we couldn't get rid of our Ghosts of Christmas Past by any other means. It's not so easy to empty your bucket, that's the trouble, especially when you're the ripe old age of twenty-eight. Rupert's bright idea to stage an exorcism turned out to be a mistake, because everyone took offence when we started reading the Lord's Prayer in a meaningful manner and chucking incense about. Afterwards I never stopped apologising, especially to the dog.

So now I live with Nick; Rupert's with someone called Gemma. It's all very new and lovely for all four of us, and Jumbly seems okay. The trouble is, despite all we've been through, we have no idea how to prevent the same business recurring – not without resorting to brainwashing, anyway. 'How's your bucket?' I ask Rupert discreetly when we see each other. 'Brim full,' he says with a shrug. 'I told Gemma off for going on about buckets all the time yesterday. I got confused and thought she was you. It never ends, does it?'

Year Zero, I call it. The perpetual fond hope that you can start a fresh, blank sheet, new calendar, while really you are forever tailed by the cast of *Truly, Madly, Deeply*, just waiting for the chance to muscle in. One's only consolation is that one is surely cropping up reciprocally in other people's lives, quite far away, without knowing a thing about it. 'You analyse things too much, that's your trouble, and you've never really appreciated my Barbies,' Jeremy says unfairly to his newest love, and *bing-bong*, Avon calling, it's Suzanne at the door. 'Remember me?' I say, as I enter. 'And marvellous news, Jeremy,' I add, as I unzip my suitcase in the hallway. 'I've taken up the trumpet. Want to hear?'

Anything You Can Do

Ruth Shabi

By the year 2000, he said, I'll be a company director. And I'll be nearly forty, I thought, with those dreadful saggy breasts like oranges in socks.

We met at a Christian Union coffee morning.
He went for an argument. I went for the free jammy dodgers.
It was my second day at university. I was homesick.
You one of them? he said.
I shook my head and tried to swallow a mouthful of biscuits.
And failed.
When I'd finished coughing, he asked me out.
We went to the Student Union bar.
His name was Mark. He came from Leicester. His mum was a dinner lady. His dad was a foreman at a pickle factory. He was the first one in his family to go to University. And he was never going back.

I told him my dad was in sewage.
Actually he was a chemical engineering consultant.
We spent the night crammed into my single bed.
He said I was sophisticated.
I sniggered.

Anything You Can Do

No really, he said, I've never met anyone who uses phrases like 'not quite compos mentis' before.

I said, I thought that was how everyone described their granny.

Before long I was in love and seeing us together for ever.

But he was seeing my roommate.

She was Irish with a mane of flame red hair, alabaster skin and green, gold-flecked eyes with a dreamy, far-away look.

She was short-sighted.
I kicked her out. Then Mark dumped her.
On the rebound, I bumped into James. A mature philosophy student with a wall eye and a silver Blue Peter Badge.

He introduced me to garlic and together we did runners from Indian restaurants.
It was daring and exciting.
But it couldn't last. I was overdrawn from going back and paying the bills.
I meant to let him down gently.
I ended up snogging his best friend.
In front of him.
The next day someone pushed the shredded pieces of a photo of me under my door.
James was nowhere to be found.
His best friend said, he's probably topped himself.
Actually, he'd been arrested for non-payment of a tandoori chicken massala, portion of special fried rice, sag aloo, two pints of lager and three

poppadoms. (They waived the coffee and After Eight mints.)

He got off with a fine.
I failed my first year exams.
I spent the summer running between the library and a night shift at a frozen pea factory.
Mark sent a good luck card from a Youth Hostel in Amsterdam.
It worked.
In the second year I moved into a damp, mouse-infested house with four girls who were allergic to cleaning.

Mark gave me a box of Flash powder for Christmas.

In the spring I met a chemistry student called Paul who had eleven older sisters and drove a MG Midget. Even though he dressed like a biker.

In the third year we shared a flat.
We had a dinner party to celebrate the end of finals.
Mark bought six bottles of Asti and everyone was sick. Except me.
Till the next morning when I watched Tiswas and Chris Tarrant put a kipper in a lemon mousse.

Mark stayed on to do a post-graduate teaching certificate and have an affair with his tutor. He said she was the most sophisticated woman he'd ever met.

What do you mean? I said.
She has a drinks cabinet, he said, with drinks in.

Paul landed a job in an American bank. Coincidentally, his uncle was a director of the firm.
He told me he was moving to New York in the autumn.
It breaks my heart to leave you, he said.
Take me with you, I said.
I can't, he said.
And left without even kissing me goodbye.
I moved into a bedsit and paid the rent with a succession of temping jobs.
They lasted anything from a week to ten days. Or as long as it took employers to find out I couldn't type.

Then I became a media Executive.

I sold space in the small ads on the *Balsal Heath Chronicle*.

I thought my luck had changed when the editor called me in.

Did you come up with this? he asked, pointing to an Easter advertorial for chair-lifts with the headline, 'I thought I'd never see upstairs again, but on the third day, I rose again.'

Yes, I said proudly.
You're sacked.

Mark suggested I try marketing. He'd ditched the tutor and the post-graduate degree for a job at Procter & Gamble.

I wrote to Sainsburys. They hired me on the strength of

composing their first letter of application in verse.

Not the ideal qualifications for a trainee Store Manager in Streatham.

I lasted nine and three-quarter months.

Then I met Jonathan. He was tall and handsome and he made me laugh. I'd decided to try my hand at advertising. He was in it up to his Armani-framed eyeballs.

After two weeks I had a job as a trainee copywriter. Coincidentally at the agency where Jonathan worked.

A year later I won an award and Jonathan asked me to marry him.
Happy ever after, I thought.
Till I caught him hoovering in a Laura Ashley dress.
The engagement ring paid for six months' rent on a flatshare in Turnpike Lane.
Then I met Robert. He knocked me over with his trolley in Safeways.
He was an analyst in the City.
Three months later I moved into his Chelsea mews house.
He worked all hours. So did I.
He got broody. I got promotion.
One night we had a row about milk bottle tops and he shut my arm in the bathroom door.
I'm so sorry, he said, it was an accident, I'd never hurt you on purpose, I love you, you know that, don't you?

Of course, I said.

A year later I bumped into Mark on Charing Cross Road. I had three stitches above my right eye.

Why don't you leave? he said.
Because I have nowhere to go, I said.
The next day he came and collected me. He told Robert he'd get him the sack if he tried to stop me.

I didn't even ask where we were going.
It was a friend's place. He was abroad for a year.
Mark made me toast and Marmite and left.
I wolfed it down.
Then threw it up.
I changed jobs.
I changed my hair.
I even changed my wardrobe.
But I still made myself sick.
Mark took me out for meals. He didn't think I was eating enough.
One day I overheard two girls in the street.
I don't get it, one of them said, is it a bloke or a girl?
They were talking about me.
A month later Mark's friend came back.
I put an offer on a flat in Notting Hill. The balcony was bigger than the bedroom and the bathroom was in a cupboard under the stairs.

Don't buy it, Mark said. Marry me. I've always known you were the one, right from the beginning, it was just never the right time.

Nor is it now, I said.

Nine months later he married a jewellery designer, called Caroline Palmer-Burke.
She had a seventeenth-century drinks cabinet, with vintage Armagnac in it.
We didn't speak for two years.

Then one morning he rang from a marketing convention in Prague. It was three thirty.
I'm a Dad, he slurred, I have a son.
Congratulations, I said.
It could have been you.
I know, I said.
A month later I moved.
From Creative Group Head to Creative Director.
From throwing things up to keeping things down.
By the time I was forty, I had my own agency and a house in Islington.
I had it all. Right down to the Alessi designed, Millennium Dome egg cosy.
In fact, the only thing I didn't have were those dreadful saggy breasts like oranges in socks. They just weren't me.

Dogs of Athens

Elspeth Barker

It was in Athens airport that I saw them first. They sat close together, very upright on their airport chairs, all knitting. Or were they all knitting? As I walked past it seemed out of the corner of my eye as though only one was knitting and the others were straightening the wool, holding the ball, but each taking her turn with the needles. Three ancient crones, wrapped in black. The three fates, Clotho, Lachesis and something. Why couldn't I remember the third one's name? It is depressing to survive for fifty years only to begin to forget things you have always known. 'Well,' says the voice in the back of my head, 'if only you hadn't drunk so much ouzo at Iraklion before you got on the plane things might be different.' 'Rubbish' I riposte. 'Flying is awful, crazy, degrading to human dignity. Remember Icarus drowning in the sea we've just crossed. There are warnings everywhere and we should take some notice.' 'Flying is the safest form of transport' says the voice. It says this often. 'Qantas has never lost a passenger,' it adds. 'What's Qantas got to do with flying Crete to Athens, or Athens to London, come to that?' I demand. I peer anxiously at the three fates, for tomorrow is another flying day. They ignore me, intent on their skeins of orange wool. Ravelling and unravelling. May the

Lord preserve us. Anyway, I have outwitted them for now.

I become aware that there are a number of cheerful dogs about, apparently unattached, trotting around the concourses, greeting pilots and vigorously enjoying the business of international arrivals and departures and casual disposal of airport food. How they smile and swish their tails; east, west, dogs are best and I am missing mine. Tomorrow I will see them. Today and now there is the hotel and then Christina.

I didn't know Christina very well although I'd seen her on and off over many years. Back in England it had seemed a good idea to stop over one night in Athens, meet, have fun. Christina hadn't actually sounded very enthusiastic down the phone, but her laconic and curiously well-preserved Texan drawl had often misled me. Now she was in hospital and I'd no idea what was wrong. She had sent a message to the hotel saying 'Come this minute, bored, bored, bored'. The hospital was up in the hills outside Athens and I was pleased to have discovered the bus station and the bus despite the intense pall of mid-afternoon heat and the major handicap of my 5th century BC Attic Greek. One of the people I had accosted for directions had insisted in only slightly American English that no one had used the rough breathing since 400 AD. That wasn't going to stop me.

As the suburbs fell away the bus gathered speed into dusty scrubland. The sky hung heavy and dull over slopes littered with unfinished breeze-block structures; in the hazed light they seemed like ruined temples, parched and skeletal. I looked forward to the cool of evening and the hotel roof garden where I might sip a Bloody Mary or two and gaze out at the ghostly Parthenon. I realised that not knowing what was wrong with Christina had no relevance; she probably wouldn't tell me anyway. If she even knew. She had a dismissive attitude to the woes of the body. I remembered her galloping through the woods on a huge grey horse, her skirts bundled up round her thighs, one broken arm in plaster and sling. She admitted to hangovers; nothing much else. And she disposed of hangovers with a slosh of brandy in the morning's second cup of coffee, followed by a spot more on the hour throughout the day. Despite her alcoholic intake, or perhaps because of it, she was able to make a reasonable living from freelance journalism, even contriving to write satirical pieces on London social life from her Athens apartment. She was consistently unkind to her lovers who never lasted more than a week or two. She would shout at them in public places; if one had really irritated her she would pick him up in a sort of fireman's hoist, sling him over her shoulder and carry him down the street. I wondered now whether I even liked her, whether this visit might not be a wretched mistake. But beyond the drinking and ranting she was funny and generous and I admired the relish she took in her odd, lonely life.

The hospital was huge and parts of it were still being built. The hillside was gouged with quarry workings, and great grey bulldozers and cranes and diggers toiled slowly back and forth, changing places, revolving, realigning in a complex and enigmatic pavane. Dust thickened the air and clouded out the sky; the colour had leached from the landscape, leaving it lunar and featureless. A no place. I thought of the word Utopia and its literal meaning of no place and how strange it is that this no place is always taken to be a desirable one.

Shining rivers of grey vinyl wound my way to Christina's room. I hesitated at the doorway, scanning the four beds. She wasn't there. Then 'Hey DUDE!' shrieked the weird person at the far end by the window. Christina was in disguise; she had dolled herself up as some kind of invalid Country-and-Western lady. Her hair hung down in blonde ringlets, her décolleté nightdress bore a huge pink satin bow just beneath the bust, strongly suggestive of Easter eggs. Over it she wore a pink feather boa, wispily attached to a fluffy angora bed jacket. The boa flipped about, involving itself with a dangling tube hooked up to Christina's left arm. God, I thought, it's a blood transfusion. My Bloody Marys made a swift and shameful appearance in my mind; lined up on a silver tray, they reeled into darkness. 'So what's the matter with you?' I demanded, sounding bossy and curt, cutting through Christina's babble about the *awesome* horror of hospital food. She was making me feel pedantic and English; she was making me hold tightly onto my handbag handles and sit with my feet in symmetrical parallel. 'Nothing much'; she sipped some water or possibly vodka. 'I had a pain in my stomach but it's gone now. They just won't let me out yet because they want to do some tests. Anyhow I'll lose some weight.' I felt reassured by this non-reply and told her about a recent visit to an English casualty ward where I overheard a doctor interviewing a youth behind closed curtains.

Doctor: 'So you have taken a number of tablets. Did you mean to kill yourself?'
Youth: 'Dunno, maybe not really, don't know.'
Doctor, keenly: 'Ever thought of cutting your wrists?'
Youth: 'No.'
Doctor: 'Do you have a garden shed?'
Youth: 'What?'
Doctor: 'A garden shed with weedkiller in it. Do you have access to weedkiller?'
Youth: 'No. For goodness' sake, what is this?'

Doctor: 'Are there firearms in your house? In an unlocked cupboard?'
Youth: 'Please go away. Just leave me alone.'
Doctor: 'So you haven't been tempted to shoot yourself?'
Youth: 'Oh fuck off.' He begins to sob.

Christina enjoyed this tale and laughed a lot. An eyelash detached itself and drifted down, iridescent and eddying in the late afternoon light. I remembered the harbour at Réthímnon and the kingfisher; it dipped back and forth among the boulders of the sea barrier, brilliant against a sullen, windy sky. Off it flew westward and all its colour was quenched into blackness before the pallid spot of the sun. The sea was swollen, pounding and dragging the shingle, the cafés were deserted, the tables stacked, the umbrellas furled. The melancholy of the changing season whined through the wind's skirmishes and the groan of the shifting shingle. All things are passing.

Christina was staring at me; I felt a pang of terror. Her eyes seemed to have receded into her skull; she gazed out as though from a cavern, withdrawn from the rest of the world, unreachable. And then she was back, complaining about the nurse who had confiscated her vodka bottle from her sponge bag, addressing her as Little Lady. 'Bloody puritanical Yanks,' she said. 'I'd be better off in a Greek hospital. Anyhow I've a story to tell you too. I've been thinking about this a lot since I've been in here. Maybe it's the best thing that's happened to me; or maybe not the best, but the thing I've liked most.'

Once upon a time Christina lived in Chicago. She was fourteen years old and her parents' marriage had just broken up, so that she and her mother had come from Texas to live with her grandmother. Christina hated it;

she missed her old home and her father and her friends, and most of all she missed her ballet lessons. Her mother promised that when they were more settled she could take them up again, but Christina didn't believe her. Like everything else here, promises were nothing, air and water. Rudolf Nureyev had recently defected and was coming to dance in Chicago. They had promised tickets for this but of course nothing had been done and now there were no tickets left. She felt intense panic at the real facts of time passing and having nowhere to practise; she was getting taller everyday and could soon be too tall to be allowed into ballet class. Or too fat, for she was bored and lonely and she ate too much. She seemed incapable of sitting down without having to eat simultaneously. Partly to avoid sitting down, and partly to make herself more miserable after school each day she would walk for hours in the bitter late winter winds. Or was it early spring? The snow had gone, but the sky remained colourless, and the buildings were grey and the waters of the great lake were grey, whisked to a constant mean turmoil by the crazy, buffeting winds. Air, water, nothing and noise, aircraft, sirens, traffic, fog horns, construction work, wind booming round the corners of the blocks.

So there Christina went, trudging along in her tight red woolly hat and her unmatching gloves, her winter trousers and boots. She dragged her soles along the concrete walkway by the lake, head down, doubled over against the roaring, idiot enemy. Her eyes stung and her chilblains itched. In the near distance a dark figure was moving rapidly, purposefully, towards her. A man. She peered round; there was no one else in sight. Her heart began to thump; God, she prayed, if you don't let him kill me, I'll stop going on these stupid walks. A flight of geese rose shrieking off the lake and passed in formation high above her, darkening the sky with omen. Their wings creaked as they went. Now the man confronted her; he stood still. Christina stood still. He wore a black cloak which puffed and billowed towards her, as if to envelop her. Speechless she stared at him, and the breath caught in her throat. It was Nureyev. He swept off his floppy black cap and bowed in a deep curve of sinuous grace. Her eyes still fixed on his face, Christina sank into a curtsey. Their gloved hands clasped as he raised her to her feet. Then they walked on in their opposite directions. 'And I didn't look back,' Christina concluded, triumphant, glowing. But a moment later her eyelids drooped and the colour had faded from her cheeks. 'I'm really sorry but I have to take a rest,' she said. 'I've had it.' I thought then that she meant she was exhausted; perhaps she did. I kissed her goodbye and I went. 'And I won't look back,' I said. She died that evening, but I didn't know this until I was back in London. I sat out then on my balcony in sultry October dusk and watched the planes stacking and sliding past the pinnacles of Westminster Cathedral and I thought of Christina and the crones and the dogs of Athens, sleeping by their own cathedral, littered in shaggy heaps about its glassy forecourt. I remembered a flower seller appearing in the early morning square, making his way round the café tables. In seconds the dogs were up and barking; they saw him off and returned to their slumbers. Later I saw them dispersed through the streets, sleeping again by dark shop doorways. At the airport they were busy as before, seeking companionship with no great urgency, amiable and bright of eye. The three crones sat knitting in their row of chairs and one of them dropped the orange ball of wool. It rolled out across the floor and a sheepdog bounded towards it. I moved fast to intercept it but it had gone. I could not tell whether the dog had seized it, the woman had picked it up or someone had kicked it off under the chairs. In my head there was an image of a pomegranate rolling across mosaic tiles and a hand outstretched to catch it, the hand of a person unseen, something from a half forgotten poem. So now, back in London, I sit clutching my handbag and staring at the sky and trying to make patterns out of memories and words and nothing at all fits.

Guatemala Moon

Clare Bayley

Soon after his birth, Oswaldo's grandmother predicted that he would one day go to the moon. But it was not for many, many years that the old Mayan woman's outlandish prediction became true, and by that time she, along with Oswaldo's mother, father, uncle, aunt, three brothers, two sisters and several cousins, was long dead. Dead, but not buried, since the army never returned the bodies to the village where they had lived.

That had happened one afternoon, and because it happened on that particular afternoon, Oswaldo was spared. He was twelve years old, dressed in a smaller version of the red trousers and striped shirt that all the men of the village wore. His mother had sent him down the valley with a sack of maize. He had not yet reached his destination when he was overtaken by his neighbour and cousin, screaming and sobbing as she skidded down the hillside behind him, her legs and ankles being ripped by stones and thorns. As she drew level with Oswaldo, she gathered him up in her arms and they skidded on together. Between gasps she shouted at him, 'They've taken them all! Your family has gone! The whole village is gone!'

Afterwards, Oswaldo spent much mental effort trying to understand why they had all gone, and he had not. It couldn't have been because he was so young, because that did not save even his littlest sister, whom he remembered only as a bulge in the sling on his mother's back, which sometimes wailed and periodically sent up a head, crumpled and befuddled by sleep, but with focusing, bright eyes.

In later life, as he began to know something of politics and governments, Oswaldo racked his memory to dredge up some evidence that his father was involved in the *campesino* movement, but there also he drew a blank. Oswaldo's memories were frustratingly irrelevant, he thought. He could remember his grandmother, a rumpled heap of exquisitely embroidered, finely woven cloths, always sitting in front of a loom. He remembered her great, rough fingers bedecked with yellow metal rings, pointing at Oswaldo and telling him he would go to the moon one day.

He could remember distinctly a patch of arum lilies between the houses, and how he and his brother used to take their heads off and wear them as hats. And he remembered the day that he and his brothers and sisters discovered a sackful of wood shavings which fell in long, pale spirals and bounced like springs when you shook them. But none of this helped him understand what happened to them all.

When his neighbour took him in and they moved to the town, he stopped wearing the red trousers and embroidered collars he was used to, and adopted instead the international disguise of T-shirt and jeans. He learned to clean shoes and boots for a living, applying the polish with small, stained fingers which worked it well into the scuffs and scratches of the leather, then burnished it with brushes and rags. He teamed up with his cousin's cousin, an older boy of seventeen, who lent him the brushes but kept almost all of the *quetzales* that the two of them earned.

The main square was a good place for business because it was where the buses arrived from all over the country, disgorging potential customers right to him. But a few years of being a shoe-shine boy was not getting Oswaldo any closer to the moon, and nor was it getting him any closer to the girls, which was a thing of far greater significance to him then. As Oswaldo hung around the scruffy little square, diving for the feet of any tourists or rich-looking people that crossed it, he realised that the reason the girls who crossed his path shied away from him was more to do with his boot-polish black fingers than anything personal about him they disliked.

Oswaldo began to notice that the boys who worked the buses got the chance to touch the waists of the girls and women as they bundled them on board. Then he realised that the women even sought the bus boys out, smiling and flirting in the hope that they would get a seat on the bus. Soon enough, Oswaldo himself began to work on the buses, and he felt quite superior, leaving the square and the other shoe-shine boys behind.

His job was to hustle the passengers and all their baggage onto the bus, take their money and attend to the driver: feeding him with Coca-Cola and cigarettes, procuring slices of watermelon for him, looking out to see how close the edge of the road was when they passed other buses on narrow bends – hurrying, harrying, running and watching all day long.

His first job took him as far away from his home village and his cousins as he could go. The route went up the hell road leading into the mountains in the west of the country, where the bus could go no faster than a brisk walk, and the track was pure, fine dust a foot deep in the dry season, and rich, axle-deep mud in the rainy season. When the mud came above the axle in the wet season, the bus did not run and Oswaldo didn't get paid. So Oswaldo would always encourage his driver to attempt the journey whatever the weather.

The bus set off at four o'clock in the morning in the total darkness and quick, sharp cold of the mountains. In the light of the headlights Oswaldo would see small groups of men and women huddled beside the road, swaddled against the cold in wraps and shawls and hats. He treated these Indians with a breezy distance which felt like shyness but bordered on disrespect. He was only vaguely aware that even if his mother and grandmother came back to him now, he would not be able to talk to them in their jerky Indian language. He had forgotten it all.

He threw all his energies into doing his job well, and being popular with the ladies. His wage was small, but he supplemented it with a discretionary gringo tax, applied systematically to all the eager-looking, sunburned faces which were to be seen sitting squashed among, yet towering over, the other passengers.

Because of his quickness and assiduity, Oswaldo gained a reputation among the bus-drivers, and soon was offered a job with a better wage for a richer bus company on faster, fitter roads which ferried travellers, traders and visiting relatives from the centre of the country down to the great lake.

Oswaldo could really prove himself as that turquoise and green bus hurtled along the steep roads, with medallions and Madonnas swinging, plastic streamers flapping, dust and hot air blowing in through the open windows. He made sure there were always latino pop songs blasting out of the tape machine to help the passengers forget their discomfort and their troubles for the four hours of the journey. He could often be seen moving down the central aisle of the bus, waving a wad of tattered bank notes in the air and singing along in his strong and just about melodic voice. It made the women giggle, the men smirk, and the smallest children stare in awe.

Soon Oswaldo was well-known all along the route, and there were girls the length of it who would stop their work when they heard the rumble of an approaching bus, and run down the road to catch Oswaldo's special smile as it flashed by, each one imagining she was the only one. So Oswaldo really felt that he was getting somewhere. He fixed his attention only on the onward momentum, which he in part controlled, and loved all the motion and commotion.

But in truth, the further and the faster Oswaldo hurtled, the more he was staying in the same place. Through the window of the bus his life was built up of half-seen, unfinished actions: the machete raised to chop a coconut, and never brought down; the laughter of the women, but never the joke itself; the bowl of water thrown, but never the splash of landing. Oswaldo was pleased to live this life without causes or effects, and perhaps it was the only life he could lead then.

As for love, he restricted it to the fleeting smiles of the *muchachas* along his route. An early excursion into the world of the flesh had left him with a burning, oozing crotch for three days, and taught him that sometimes a distant flirtation is preferable to the consequences of reality. A shadow in the deepest recess of his memory confirmed his suspicion that love meant pain of one sort or another, and so he avoided it.

Besides, Oswaldo knew he was destined for greater things than that. He remembered his grandmother's words, but found them confusing. Americans had already been on the moon by the time he was a baby, and by now were bored by it. Their sights were set higher – a machine had already been sent to Mars. Who knows where Oswaldo might end up in the next millennium? The gringos on the buses were always telling Oswaldo about the ruins of temples and cities his ancestors built longer ago than 2000 years. Some said they were modelled on the constellations, and some said they were built to receive alien space ships, but everyone agreed that Oswaldo's ancestors were the original astronomers. They knew about the stars and the planets before any gringo ever set foot on Cape Canaveral. As the year 2000 approached, their excitement about the Mayan mysteries of numbers and myths intensified. They all wanted to be close to the ancient wisdom as the world sped forwards in time, and their belief in its power was infectious.

Oswaldo began to think that his trip into space was his birthright twice over. He started to tell people about it, and especially when he was drunk, which was happening more and more frequently now. He said he was saving up to go to the US. Once there, he would present himself at the astronauts' training college and see what they would say about that. This tale caused great mirth among all who heard it, and nobody believed him at all, with the exception of one very small girl who made the eight-hour journey to and from her village each Thursday with her grandmother.

Every week they piled onto the bus with huge bundles of *huipiles*, squares of cloth and little bags that they had woven for the tourists at the weekly market. The little girl always asked Oswaldo, with shining eyes and a slight flush of shyness, when exactly he was going to the moon, and whether she could come with him. Her ancient grandmother, meanwhile, laughed with gummy affection, winking at the other passengers, and Oswaldo felt a prick of humiliation that his 'savings' had once again been blown on cane liquor.

One Thursday, the little girl clambered onto the bus at the customary place, but this time carrying an unusually large bundle, and without her grandmother to accompany her. The bus was crowded, but Oswaldo took the trouble to make sure the little girl found somewhere to squat down, squashed underneath the dashboard near the driver's feet. Throughout the journey Oswaldo and the child exchanged smiles and winks as they usually did. But when the bus finally reached its destination, after all the passengers and their luggage had been disgorged, the little girl remained.

'You'll lose your pitch, *niña*,' advised Oswaldo in a friendly sort of way.

'No,' replied the girl quite solemnly. 'Today I'm coming home with you because my grandmother is dead. And we are going to the moon.'

Oswaldo was dumbfounded. He explained to the girl that he couldn't look after her, and she couldn't come home with him, because he had nowhere to live, just one dirty old room, and no wife to take care of her and cook her food. But the little girl just sat impassively among the brightly-coloured bundles of her worldly possessions, and looked Oswaldo straight in the eye.

'You must go back to your village,' he pleaded, 'your family will be waiting for you'.

'All my family are gone now,' she replied calmly. 'My grandmother was the last one left, and now she is gone.'

Oswaldo couldn't believe that the little girl didn't have any cousins at all, though her village was in an area he knew had received frequent visits from the army for as long as he could remember.

'I can't look after you. I have to work,' he said, affecting more harshness than he really felt. 'At midday the bus is going back on its route, and I'm going with it.'

The little girl said no word of protest, just looked at him, very intently. Oswaldo shrugged and walked away, leaving her squatting by the bus terminal with her bundles around her. Oswaldo went about his business with outward nonchalance, but inward nervousness. He returned back in time for the next bus journey a little earlier than usual. Sure enough, there was the little girl, sitting waiting for him.

'I have to go with the bus,' he said, defensively. She nodded, unperturbed. Oswaldo sighed.

'It's another five hours in the bus,' he warned, exaggerating slightly.

She nodded again.

'Well, I can hide you at the back of the bus, but then I am leaving you back at your village,' he said.

Not seeming to have heard the second part of the sentence, the little girl's face lit up with smiling relief. She unwrapped one of her bundles with tiny fingers, and took out of it a small and inexpertly fashioned tortilla, which she offered to Oswaldo.

'I've eaten,' he said, so she nodded and ate the tortilla herself.

He did hide her on the bus, but he didn't take her back to her village, which was quite a distance from the main road. Instead he took her to the nearest town, which was also the end of his route. Without a word but with a dark look around the brows he took her to the municipal orphanage, and left her there. She screamed and howled and raged all night until six o'clock, when she knew his bus was leaving for the return journey. Then she fell strangely quiet. She went and sat by the door, waiting expectantly. Within five minutes a haggard-looking Oswaldo reappeared. She rushed towards him, and he lifted her into the air, and from that moment on she knew she was his. The orphanage staff did not protest; they were glad to get such a noisy one off their hands.

Oswaldo refused to talk to the girl all day. He did not reassure her or admit what he was doing, but when they arrived back in his town, he led her to his dirty little room, and lit a paraffin lamp. 'What's your name, then?' he asked.

'Julia,' she said.

'I'm Oswaldo,' he told her, and he looked around him at the squalor and the one, stringy hammock in a hopeless way. Julia, however, knew exactly what to do. She quickly went to one of the uncluttered corners, moved aside a few empty bottles, undid a bundle and laid out a blanket.

'Goodnight Oswaldo,' she said, and fell asleep.

Normally Oswaldo would have gone out drinking at this stage in the day, but tonight he was disorientated. He sat on his hammock for a while, and thought of all the reasons why he couldn't take care of a little girl. Maybe he wasn't going to the US, but still he had things to do and places to go that you couldn't take an indigenous girl, especially when she wasn't even your child. And he couldn't leave her alone in this hovel all day long while he was riding the buses. So he would have to take her back to the orphanage, or a nunnery, or the hospital, or even the police.

But the next morning Julia was quite impervious to his threats. She tutted him in a maternal sort of way, and told him to go out and buy some more kerosene for the stove so she could make his coffee. For breakfast she offered him one of her two remaining tortillas, and a banana she extracted from one of the bundles. Seeing this, Oswaldo went out again, and came back with some cheese and eggs which Julia cooked. As he ate she told him that he had no need to worry, because she would come with him on his bus journeys and sell her *típicos* along the route, and earn her keep that way. Oswaldo was dubious, but that morning he took her along with him and persuaded the bus-driver to let her ride without paying a fare.

But it couldn't go on this way forever. One night a week or so later, Oswaldo left Julia alone in his room and went out for a despairing drink. His usual drinking companions berated him for his recent absence, but he struck up a conversation with an old friend from the buses who told him that an American satellite TV company was looking for people, and they were prepared to train them. They bounced the beams into your home direct from the US via space, and provided all the channels you could get if you lived in Texas or California. Everyone wanted them, so the company was taking on plenty of men.

Oswaldo would never have thought of it if it hadn't been for Julia, but two days later he went along to the address given him. After a few fibs about his schooling, he landed himself a job installing and repairing dishes.

The first thing he did then was to go out and buy a small hammock for Julia, which he slung up in her corner. He also bought a broom, a second saucepan, a new shirt for himself and a hair-toggle with Mickey Mouse on it for Julia.

Oswaldo and Julia fell into a mutually satisfactory routine. Julia would come on the back of the moped the satellite company provided, carrying a bundle of *típicos* on her back. As he worked his way along the houses, she would set out her stall at a convenient point beside the road, adding slices of pineapple and peeled oranges to her repertoire. Oswaldo knew she would be quite safe, but kept an eye on her from the top of his ladder. He got used to always seeing the world from twenty feet up, and he took to singing, at the top of his voice, so the sound floated down to Julia where she sat with her wares. He got used to having Julia always in sight, always near him, chattering and laughing as they buzzed along the roads on the moped, always up and awake before him to light the stove and get the coffee on.

One day Oswaldo passed a neighbour in the street, and she stopped him.

'You need to buy some new clothes for Julia,' she said.

Pilar was a handsome woman, a little older than Oswaldo, who had been abandoned by the father of her child, who had become Julia's friend. Oswaldo had occasionally eaten in Pilar's bar as a bus boy. Then he found her a little intimidating, but when Julia and little Clementina became friends, she seemed a little softer. Pilar heard that Oswaldo had quit the buses to work for the TV company, and how he had rescued Julia and taken her into his home.

For some time Oswaldo had been aware of the need for new clothes, but was at a loss to know what to do. What did a little girl need? Should he get traditional clothes or American-style T-shirts and jeans? Would the shop-keeper laugh at him if he went in asking for clothes for a six-year-old girl? When Pilar brought up the subject, he was filled with confusion, blushed like a ripe mango, shuffled a bit and looked at the ground. Pilar burst out laughing and then suggested, 'If you give me some money, I'll buy the things Julia needs'. When he thanked her timidly, she gave him a gentle look which quite unnerved him for the rest of that day. And, indeed, for the whole of the following week.

Julia noticed his distraction, and quickly realised that

the only thing which assuaged it was talking about Pilar. So she started chattering away, telling him everything she could think of about Pilar, and a few things that she invented. She told Oswaldo that she loved Pilar more than anyone else in the world except him, and Clementina of course.

Pilar also suggested at this time that Julia should be going to school. She said that for a few *quetzales* a week she could look after Julia and Clementina when they got back from school if Oswaldo was at work, provided that Oswaldo could keep an eye on both the girls while Pilar and her mother went to the next town to order provisions for the bar. Julia and Oswaldo both agreed that this was a good idea, even though both felt sad that their special times above and below the satellite dishes were coming to an end. Julia begged Oswaldo to allow her to come up to the top of the ladder just one time before school started. Although Oswaldo protested that it was far too dangerous and difficult, both knew that he would do it.

It was the sight of an army convoy on the road that finally persuaded him. Oswaldo was working on the main transmitter for the area, a giant pylon festooned with dishes and radio transmitters. It wasn't that the army would take any notice of Julia by the side of the road, or of him up the transmitter, but he just suddenly decided he would rather have Julia up there with him. He shimmied down to the ground, picked Julia up, put her on his back, and clambered up the frame. She was as light as a lizard but with strong little arms and legs which gripped him securely. When they reached the top, she looked around in amazement and delight at the bird's eye view of everything. Then she put her head back and gazed into the blue sky, where a nearly-full moon was palely visible in the East. Unbeknown to either Julia or Oswaldo, at that very moment a space craft was winging its way past the moon on a mission to another more distant planet. But it was so far away, it was invisible to the eye.

'Oswaldo, will you marry Pilar?' enquired Julia, and Oswaldo laughed heartily. As he worked he broke into song, and Julia joined in, giggling excitedly. From the top of the transmitter, their voices rang out. Distracted in his work, Oswaldo was clumsier than usual. He never knew, but perhaps somewhere up in the stars his grandmother knew. For a few, brief, panic-stricken moments in the control room at Houston, their voices broke through, blocking the air-to-ground communication of the space craft. It was a quirk of technology that the Air Chief Marshal in control of the mission would lengthily explain at several enquiries and many dinner-parties over the following year. By the time of the dinner parties, he could laugh about it. But for the full sixty-five seconds before the technicians managed to rescue the situation, he sat in paralysed horror, shaking, sweating and pale like someone in the throes of malaria listening to those unknown, raucous voices.

Oswaldo, unaware, finished his job, and together he and Julia clambered down to the ground. At the bottom, Julia had that far-away, all-knowing look on her small face. She gazed fixedly at the dim moon in the bright sky, and she said, 'We don't need to go there now, do we?' Then she smiled at Oswaldo with something of the old wisdom of his dead grandmother, and he smiled back, as they turned and walked together back towards the TV company moped.

Exposure

Helen Cleary

A raw vine of tattered wallpaper borders the open door. Shutters hang lazily, milling about the window like a straggle of adolescents littering the pavement outside some local shop. Chewing gum, never talking. Even the sea is sulking in the distance. This light is no good. Jenny wishes it would either be sunny or just rain, just do something.

But then she catches her mother's metallic hair as it suddenly dazzles reflection. Fingers tense around the lens.

Strange to think they are pulled together by a mere twist of DNA. All of them.

'*Mami* Sue, *Mami* Sue.' Little voices squeak from between garden tree trunks. Jenny's mother has to obey. She doesn't get to be Grandma often. She smiles her special smile at Jen, casts it out and Jen hooks it with gratitude.

She coaxes the lens into focus, the fingers of her left hand making like an owl eye. Do they mind? She suddenly remembers being frozen herself, caught by a boyfriend's camera forcing a hybrid smirk-cum-donkey lip-curl, not knowing him enough for the pose to be natural.

DNA reproduces itself. A helter-skelter of mimicry. A genetic echo. There's a theory... something about crystals. Like the very earliest of crystals, DNA learnt to replicate itself, strand upon strand, snow upon snow. This was the beginning. She likes patterns, repetition, tessellations of white and shadow. She has constantly sought to capture them.

A scream from outside swoops in, a magpie into a songbird's nest. That brittle screech unique to toddlers... although they are little girls, three or four years old now. One belonging to each of her two brothers. But Jenny focuses on this brother, Andy, and his eldest daughter sitting beneath him. A portrait. The girl's bare foot slaps onto cool floor, her second toe curls into a tiny island of missing tile. A gibbous moon of white toenail rests on the jagged terracotta edge, giving the plump, pinking toe a pig-in-a-sty look. Jen can't get this, not with black and white film. Anyway, feet are impossible to photograph successfully.

'Come on Angelou, bet you can't do this one.' Boy emerges from man, like a smoke ring being blown through a smoke ring. 'That was my big brother, a grown man, challenging a little girl,' thinks Jenny. He peddles a tune on his guitar. Jenny wonders if he has ever grown up. He's handsome. Both her brothers are. She's not supposed to think this. Andy has walnut-brown skin, something of Richard Gere in his white hair and emperor nose. His hands are big, the thumbs bleached, chiselled out of granite and so strong. The nails too broad, like inflatable dinghies stuck at the bend of a river. There is something repulsive about his nails, especially now he's tanned; they are yellow-white like marrow in bone. If someone did a caricature of these fingers they would splay at the ends like frog toes. But she likes frogs.

'You're *so* competitive, Andy. She's only nine.'

'Aw, c'mon Jen,' he says. A slice of song, a mantra he

often wedged at her when she herself was a little girl pestering him.

'Ten,' pipes Angelou. The girl's azure eyes linger adoringly on Jenny, her *'tantine'*. Is that right? Somehow it sounds better than 'auntie'. More familiar yet sophisticated at the same time. Jenny raises her camera, framing the puppy-dog look, distancing it. She doesn't want this unconditional, undiscerning love. It cloys.

'Come on! One more tune. You have to keep it up, you're so good,' manages Jen.

The ting of register as the little girl translates and looks to her father as if he can telepathically hear her head-mumbled unpicking of words. From English to French and then back again in her own interior voice, Angelou savours the meaning of this praise.

Angelou has translucent, delicate skin, like the film that covers a shelled boiled egg, and a rich skein of copper-amber hair. She starts to play. An ancient French sound fills the room. This child makes Jenny think of fairytale books and Rapunzel. Trapped. Feral. Why hadn't she brought colour film too? Beautiful purply lips blowing Os in concentration. The tongue inside, too human, pushing against teeth. It's definitely a strange choice of instrument. Little Breton girls dance on lacquered wood. They seem, well ... so girlish. Caught forever at a fancy dress party. Doomed to wear traditional costume for the rest of their lives, even though doughy breasts will sag and hips creak apart. Euch. Jen shivers.

She's a strange child, Angelou, and is probably gifted.

'How about that one about the lake or the river, y'know, somewhere in France ... erm, oh, whatsit called?' asks Jen. Her encouragement is raw, elephantine in its lumbering. Still those adoring eyes.

Her brother scowls his disapproval. 'Eh? No, let's do

"Stairway to Heaven".' Beat. 'Angelou!' The girl reluctantly returns her attention to her everyday father.

Thumb manoeuvring, as if she has just realised she's a primate, Angelou squeezes out a chord. What's the word... reversible thumbs? God, why can't she remember these things? Why is understanding science like trying to skin tomatoes hanging on a wire? But anyway, that's the difference – isn't it? It's all in the thumb. To think that to be human is to have a thumb. Maybe palmistry has some relevance, after all. Mustn't rule it out, thinks Jen. Andy's thumb, on his right hand, curves out, rebelling against nylon strings, but still manages to stroke the guitar for a tune. There's the phrase 'Rule-of-thumb', too. Her brother would probably laugh if he could hear her thoughts. He has always considered her a dreamer. He accuses her of disassociating words and scrambling pictures. But she's got a camera now.

He is often ready to laugh, his jokes quite predictable but quirky like slipping up on grapes instead of bananas. His humour shows his instinctive intelligence. He is his own kind of clever, his knowledge gathered about him. Rule-of-thumb! Like a blindfolded person navigating a room, he feels his way round a subject until he discovers how to handle it with confidence. Now, as he crouches over his guitar, she catches the V of his receding hairline. It echoes the logo on the chest of some kid's superhero costume.

Their duet jangles out, teasing the window panes, but not stirring the lethargic shutters. Laughable really, Jen thinks, to watch father and child chewing tongues over a '70s classic. Painfully slow. Jurassic. But they are getting it right.

What was that song... a lake or river, some region of France? Doesn't it begin with an 'A'? Dancing.

Romance. Jen had heard it last year, on another French holiday, further south. Lucy had sung it. Pied-piping to herself, she had been charmed by her own voice, stumbling along mesmerised by her own notes, half-forgetting the lyrics but then collecting them like a trail of breadcrumbs deliberately left to show the way. Yeah, she didn't quite know the tune or the words. It was charming, Jenny had to admit. Lucy had sung and shaved curls of parmesan over tuna fish and lettuce. '*Ça suffit. Alors, la salade Niçoise!*' she had trilled, feigning a Piaf warble as she returned to her song. Lucy had been the hardest to get on with somehow. So convinced of her own charm . . . you could tell because she was so insistently modest.

The group of friends had eaten outdoors beneath a fig tree, pungent rotting fruit at their feet. The huge leaves overhead stirred occasionally. Punkah wallahs. Stars slipped between the foliage like frogs diving. Frogs again. France. Jenny had drunk too much wine and obsessed over Lucy's love life; was he really good enough for her, shouldn't she be a bit more assertive, was it made to last? Really Jenny wanted Lucy's boyfriend back. Single. He had been Jenny's friend first and always good for a laugh.

The shrieks from outside come closer. A deep-throated chuckle sneaks underneath other noises like a dog under a gate. The two little ones are a closed deal, a recalcitrant duo, linked by their naughtiness, but much tamer apart. They have signed a pact without even knowing it. They bat intelligently between French and English, detecting immediately the nationality of their audience. They will not waver from this; it's an unwritten rule. This is their club, this easy fooling with language. No one else can join. They would not have the ready flair. Jenny hears bubbles of childish French float on the heavy air; they pop at her envy.

Now she hears her stepfather somewhere in the garden. He is telling stories and herding the two little girls around the lawn. 'Yes, I think spiders are terribly tasty. Let's hunt some out.' (Pause, for effect!) 'You know, I think I even prefer them to crisps.' Pairs of eyes widen. Pulse. Neither want to be thought gullible, but *Grandpapi* is too old for jokes and pranks. 'Yes, they are wonderfully crunchy, especially those speckly ones – they have a very particular flavour. Quite an acquired taste. Rather nutty. A bit like Twiglets. And those teenie weenie red ones? They are very sweet.' He smacks his lips. '*Délicieux!* But you know, the problem with eating spiders is that their legs get stuck between your teeth.' At this one head nods, of course! Then the other dances her curls too; she has got a licence from her cousin now. They begin to seek earnestly in the bushes, not afraid of spiders in the slightest.

'Yes, never get caught without a toothpick when you're eating spiders,' says *Grandpapi*.

In another part of this undone house is Babette, Andy's partner. Not 'wife' or 'girlfriend'. She is shelling peas. Her ears always registering the sounds of her children against background noise, like those digital signs on top of city buildings that flick up the time, then the temperature, the time, then the temperature. Jenny is afraid of her, muted by respect. She is academic but a mother. Full of love as well as wisdom. Jenny can see Babette's self-assurance snugly sat on a mat inside that grown-up body, strong against anything. This woman is too big in her goodness, all-roundedness and unthinkable intelligence. Before all of this Jenny feels watched, known. Like Babette has seen back-to-back reels of Jenny's adolescent mewling and puking at various unfunny teenage parties, or has taped every utterance of pitiful angst – a friend stealing the limelight, a zit that simply won't go. Every middle-class chip seems to jump from Jenny's shoulders and dance before Babette's eyes chanting, 'Look at me! Look at me!'

They never ask if she has a 'boyfriend' (not 'partner'). Or 'girlfriend' for that matter! But then they wouldn't. She must have a mild whiff of promiscuity about her armpits. They don't want this knowledge, not until she too settles into a partnership and finds herself pregnant. Then, suspects Jenny, she will be drawn in at last.

Click! Jenny has caught her brother, the power in his back, the crook of arm against curve of guitar. A small ghostlike hand on accordion keys tilts upwards into the shot. Click!

'Oooh!' gasps Angelou, as if Jenny had magicked a bunch of flowers from her sleeve.

Jen changes her range. Focuses out and beyond. Away.

Is he in love, her brother? Still – after the childcare, the tussles, the moments of hatred that must have passed between them? Just the night before, Jen thought she glimpsed love. It simmered and peeped out, a chord of silver around the mass of clouds. Babette's eyes had rumbled, then shimmered, and a coil of tiger's energy came undone inside her as she pulled at the big man's sleeve and softly spoke to him in her mild Breton accent, 'C'mon. The night . . . so beautiful. I'll race you to the sea.' They swam! Swam in the middle of the night! She must have gently coaxed the bulk of her brother, who doesn't float easily, into the inky soup of water. Radiant bodies must have foreshortened in the endless dark, bumping towards each other.

This wasn't what she saw her peers do. They worked in formation, eating dinner together at Pizza Hut, turning up at parties at the same time and always leaving together. They wore carefully chosen clothes that somehow complemented each other; bought each other androgynous perfumes with designer labels. Everything was clean, neat, uncomplicated. Their smiles were a little wan. Nothing *really* glittered.

Andy couldn't resist Babette's call. They had gone out into the sludge of night, he grabbing a bottle of Pernod on the way. Why did he have to drink Pernod? Such a cliché, thinks Jen. He's become so French. 'To warm us up!' he had winked.

The house seems to shift and dilate in the lens of Jenny's camera. Time passes. It has witnessed its own hurricane, this house; a wind has skewered through, ripping out walls and peeling away floorboards and tiles. Patches of concrete ooze upwards, although occasionally a new door or a repaired banister gestures a willingness to recover, to rebuild, to grow up around this scattered family and comfort it. But at the same time something eerie lives here; it moves to the sound of the surreal notes of the accordion. There are the dolls, limbs abandoned, heads twisted – holocaust-strewn carnage everywhere. Blackened with grime, they are disaster victims pictured in the aftermath. Or warriors marked with the heraldry of felt-tip wars. They wear their insignia like fallen queens and stare blankly across splintered wood and dirty terracotta. Amputees every one, just like the single socks and other oddments that are casually scattered about these rooms; objects that encourage navigational skills. Somehow, no one seems to trip up on them. This house whispers that symmetry and aesthetics are only for the shallow or inexperienced – those who haven't really lived.

Suddenly, the two babies spill into the musical spell, not heeding the adult conspiracy of hush that cushions recitals. Outside has burst indoors. They brush the air with naked shrieks of delight, clothes long abandoned. What is it about childhood that adores nudity? At the sight of these little white butt-naked bodies Jenny finds embarrassment niggling at her chest... or is it somewhere around her ears? She raises her camera too quickly. 'Snap!' The camera's sound has changed all of a sudden.

'Snap, snap!'

Jenny is trying to bottle the smell of family. *Eau de Famille*. Photos, especially of these naked girls, work hard to explain that she's at ease. Really. Somehow a photograph signals approval, acceptance or even something more casual. Unflinching. Each time she releases the shutter Jenny is saying that she hasn't really noticed their little fannies and their bare bums. But there is that feeling again. Embarrassment. You can see their unfinished muscles. They are dolphins. They have bumps where sex will sprout. From fish to land mammal. Protean. It's that feral thing again, she can almost smell the musk. Is this wrong? Do other people think like this? Till they have their own perhaps?

Babies are the produce of loving, of lust, of shared isolation. Wrapped habit, rucked bedsheets, Sunday mornings, too much wine. Or a human wail lost in the enormity of the primordial cosmos, thinks Jenny bleakly. But her handsome brother and that inscrutable French woman? Is that love? Jenny is unsure what it should look like. Shouldn't it have a red rose in its lapel, or announce itself and do a little jig, sporting bells on its shoes? Shouldn't it entertain king and court? Entertain her? Will she find her jester, whose archaic antics will never cease to keep her transfixed?

Jen's camera turns back to Andy. He grins goofily, squinting a little. Too posed. She puts the cap over her lens, places the camera gently down, feeling a bit lost now.

They were gone some time last night, swimming in the dark. A sprinkle of flirtatious laughter and sea-salt had lingered at unlocked porch doors as the rest of the family had silently closed in to fill the space.

Friends

Barbara Trapido

Dinah had been at school with Michelle and Lorraine, but that was a long time ago. Exactly thirty years ago. And in another place; in what Dinah, occasionally, in joke mode, still refers to as 'the colonies'. Dinah was never close to Michelle or Lorraine. Her best friend was Helena McKinnon, a brainy slouch who was the best company in the world. Neither were Michelle and Lorraine particularly friendly with each other. What connected the four girls was that they lived in the same suburb and caught the same bus to school every morning. Plus they were all in the sixth form art class. They were Miss Findlay's School Certificate Art girls.

'The High' was a genteel, all-female affair; a large white building on a verdant, sub-tropical hill, founded by Scottish female educationists and subsequently managed by a line of unmarried Scottish headmistresses. It strove to embody all the values of an equivalent Edinburgh academy of the years between the two world wars. Every morning Dinah and Helena would giggle together in the assembly hall as the music mistress played snatches of Handel, or Elgar, or Delius, after which the head would exhort her girls to heights of achievement and application. The girls were always ranked before her, either in 'summer' or in 'winter' uniform, though the climate was one in which the temperature never fell below 75 degrees Fahrenheit. Temperature, in those days, was always quoted in Fahrenheit. In summer, the girls wore ankle socks and biscuit cotton frocks – frocks with only one pocket to prevent any 'vulgar' girls from putting their hands in their pockets. In winter, they wore navy serge gymslips with gabardine blazers and black woollen stockings. Black velvet Alice bands were compulsory. There were 'indoor' and 'outdoor' shoes.

Lorraine was a heavy, serious-minded girl whose personality had been formed early in life and, more or less, by accident. She had been given two books by an uncle at the age of seven. One was called *Plot Outlines of a Hundred Famous Novels*, and the other was called *World's Best Paintings*. On the basis of these encyclopaedic works, she had claimed for herself the position of class intellectual and she guarded that position with zeal. In addition, Lorraine took out-of-school elocution lessons, so that she could do recitations in an accent wholly unlike the one she used for her everyday speech.

Yet it was Helena who was picked to read a passage from *The Gospel According to St Matthew* in the assembly hall on the occasion of the Governor General's visit – a circumstance which afterwards drew a heated response from Lorraine.

'I've been speaking to Miss Barnes,' she said. Miss Barnes was the drama teacher. 'We both agree that your voice production is wrong,' she said. 'In fact, Miss Barnes believes that you'll probably *have* no voice by the time you're thirty-five.'

Dinah and Helena giggled together about this. They could not imagine ever being thirty-five. Not ever. Besides, they neither of them, at that stage, had any formulated ambition. They were not driven; not like Lorraine. Dinah and Helena's termly reports always said 'could do better'. For them the purpose of school was to provide a context in which their friendship could flourish and grow.

Helena was a competent mimic and a polished entertainer. It was not surprising that Lorraine should one day come across her walking ponderously to and fro in the playground, reciting Milton's *Lycidas* in Lorraine's own elocution voice. She barged through the crowd and punched Helena four-square in the mouth. The blow almost dislodged one of Helena's incisors and left her to face her future with an oddly angled front tooth. This didn't seem to bother Helena, who was already very attractive to large numbers of young men. She was especially popular with the more senior undergraduates in the local architectural school and she spent many late nights in their company. During the daytime, her school-age male admirers would spend their lunch-hour leaning over the school gate, only to be shooed away by whichever female guardian happened to be on playground duty.

The hectic nature of Helena's nightlife meant that she was often tired at school and so, as it happened, was Dinah. Dinah was tired because she took daily doses of hayfever medicine which always made her sleepy. For this reason she and Helena contrived every possible occasion on which to skive off together to the medical room. Once there, they were required to sign a book and specify cause of incapacity. Dinah always wrote 'hayfever'. Helena entered a variety of conditions including 'sinusitis', 'period pains' and 'hypochondrial diffusions'. She spent much of her time in the medical room turning cartwheels, or doing headstands up against the walls. She was caught in action only once, by the aged head of history.

'I'm anaemic, Miss Vaisey' Helena said, having deftly

righted herself. 'I've heard it's advisable to get blood to the brain.'

After Dinah and Helena had finally passed out of 'the High'; had giggled their way one last time through 'Lord Dismiss Us With Thy Blessing', Dinah had gone straight on to university; to the Department of Fine Art. Neither Helena, nor Michelle and Lorraine, had followed her there. Helena had taken off by mail boat, to travel round Britain and Europe. She'd gone in the company of one of her architects and she wrote back wonderful letters, the first of which came on a two-metre strip torn from a scratchy loo roll. Each perforated section was stamped 'London County Council – Now Wash Your Hands'. From the British Isles, Helena had then gone on, via France and Spain, to Italy where she'd abandoned the architect for another. She'd fallen in love with a Milanese whose grandfather had designed two railway stations for Benito Mussolini, so that the trains could run on time. Helena wrote that the slow train was the one that was called the 'espresso'.

Lorraine, the self-appointed class intellectual, had surprised everyone but the maths teacher, by failing to scrape the necessary grade in maths. This disqualified her from university entrance, but it couldn't be helped. Her commitment to the arts was always such that it made her take a strong stand against maths and she had not allowed herself to assimilate any rudiment of algebra. Michelle, who had not much brain, had failed practically everything, but – thanks to her considerable drawing ability – she'd at once got a job in a downtown draughtsman's office, with her own birchwood desk and T-square.

Dinah regretted that Helena was not with her in the women's hall of residence and missed her all the time, especially when she got the head's phonecall.

'Dinah?' said the head's voice, already, after only four months, like a ghost from the distant past. 'This is Miss Phimister speaking. Do you remember me?' Dinah's first response was regression and panic; panic that the head would have at last found out which duo it was that had deliberately muddled up all the bras in the change rooms on the occasion of the inter-school swimming gala. But no, that was not it at all. What Dinah had done, it seemed, was something which gained her brownie points in the eyes of 'the High' and its staff. She had won a national essay award – the Queen Victoria Memorial Award – with her performance in the School Certificate exam. She had the highest mark in the country for her English Language essay. The subject of the essay had been 'Clothes' – one that was close to Dinah's heart, and to Helena's.

'You, Dinah,' said the head, 'have brought honour to the school.'

Dinah felt at once that Helena should have won this prize, but then Helena had not been there to write the exam. Having risen late that morning, she had tossed a coin to establish whether the exam had been scheduled for the morning or the afternoon. Heads, morning; tails afternoon. The coin had come up tails. The exam had been in the morning. Helena appeared in the lunch hour and laughed about it with Dinah, the way they laughed about almost everything. It amused them that the coin could have got it wrong.

Three weeks after the head's surprising phonecall, Dinah, home for the weekend, ran into Lorraine in the town's main shopping street. Lorraine was working as a classroom assistant in a local private prep school and had money of her own to go shopping.

'By the way,' she said, 'about that "essay prize" of yours – I've been on to the Education Department and they sent me to the government offices. I was given access to all the English Language papers, so I've seen your paper and I've seen mine. That's how I happen to know my essay got half a per cent more than yours. Yours was less controversial,' she said. 'That's why the examiners decided to give the prize to you.' Dinah completely believed Lorraine; both believed her and didn't really care. An essay prize? Half a per cent? What was the problem? The whole thing seemed utterly so-what. Dinah was on her way to buy oil brushes and a staple gun for fixing her artist's canvas to the stretchers.

Now, thirty years later, what reminds Dinah of the essay incident is that she has just met Lorraine once again – this time in an air-conditioned shopping mall, because people in Dinah's home town no longer shop in the street. They shop in conglomerate consumer palaces built of steel and glass, where the shops spill colonial heritage furniture and Persian rugs out onto the gleaming indoor walkways. Dinah has lived in England for the last twenty-seven years, but she is back on a visit to her mother. Lorraine, against a backdrop of anodyne piped music, invites Dinah, insistently, to her home. 'You must come to dinner,' she says, and her house materialises as a palatial affair with a swimming pool and a tennis court and a flunkey in a red satin cummerbund.

Lorraine's husband is unsuitably pigmentless for a climate hot as this one. He looks very like a boiled egg. An urbane boiled egg who smokes Cuban cigars. He explains at length how, having lost his vocation at theological college, he has subsequently made good in business. Lorraine, on the other hand, has made a move the other way. Having returned to education under the special rules pertaining to mature students, she has graduated *cum laude*, and now lectures in the theology department of the local university. She gives Dinah chapter and verse as the five-course meal rolls on; doctoral thesis completed, conference papers presented, articles accepted for learned publication, etcetera. The husband acts as her personal praise poet. He provides simultaneous elaboration and back-up. The couple, it appears, have one daughter, who is currently at guide camp and is eligible for prodigy status. Dinner is a smuggies' convention.

Throughout, Dinah says almost nothing. She nods her head, and nods, and nods. As she does so, it dawns on her that Lorraine wasn't telling the truth about getting access to the School Certificate essays. Good Lord! Only a total sucker could ever have believed her; believed that an unauthorised eighteen-year-old gained access to government department documents. The recognition amuses her. It gives her a welcome diversion. The other thing that diverts her is the way Lorraine's flunkey enters, as if by magic, always at precisely the appropriate moment, without appearing to have been summoned.

Dinah has worked out – just before the grape *brulée* is followed by vintage tawny port and nuts – that Lorraine summons the flunkey by means of a bell which is lodged under the carpet at her feet. It makes no sound in the dining room, but it surely must buzz in the kitchen? Dinah, back in England, is a painter. Her recent West End exhibition was a sell-out and was written up glowingly in several national broadsheets. Naturally, neither Lorraine, nor her husband, touches on what Dinah does – and any reference to Helena is evidently off-limits.

But there is, to Dinah's mild surprise, quite frequent mention of Michelle. Loraine and Michelle have become close, through the timing of their children's birth dates. They bonded, years ago, in the ante-natal class. Michelle, in the past, was never perceived as an appropriate companion for the sixth form intellectual. She was, as the head would have had it, a 'vulgar' girl for whom a two-pocket uniform would have induced unfortunate deportment. Dinah remembers her as an innocuous, silly, sharp-faced girl with a good body and a shrieky laugh. Michelle, she remembers, was sexually precocious and, throughout school, had a steady boyfriend called Jason, whom she met on the beach at weekends. Because of this, Michelle was always available on Monday mornings, to explain the mysteries of French kissing and to bare her back to show the class the white imprint of Jason's hand across her otherwise newly tanned spine.

'By the way,' Lorraine observes in parting, 'Michelle is going overseas next month and she's planning to come and see you.'

Michelle's visit to Dinah in England is arranged, long-distance, by telephone. Dinah decides to take Michelle out to dinner, since this is a woman whom she no longer really knows and Michelle might not hit it off with her husband and her two undergraduate sons who are home, with their girlfriends, for the vacation. She books a table at a restaurant in the village and arranges to meet Michelle off the train. In preparation for her night out, and because she is apprehensive, Dinah has had a new haircut and she dons the newish Annabel Harrison dress that she bought for her recent private view. Michelle arrives in traveller's scuffed white trainers which she wears with a whiter-than-white trouser suit and lots of heavy gold jewellery. It's a shock that her once beautiful, voluminous brown hair – still worn long and loose – is now bleached a fierce, peroxide yellow and rigorously flicked up into flick-ups. The major shock, however, is Michelle's personality. Or was she always like this?

Dinah finds out almost at once, thanks to Michelle's

high-speed straight-talking, that an early marriage to Jason didn't last much beyond the ante-natal class that Michelle had shared with Lorraine. Although the divorce settlement was considerable (the beach boy having been, appropriately, the son of Mr Big in popular beachwear), Michelle now has an aged provider she refers to as 'my Sugar-Daddy'. This person is both sickly and rich, and has brought Michelle to Europe, to act as his carer, all expenses paid.

'I make him spend, spend, SPEND,' Michelle says. She makes an embarrassing gesture with her right thumb and forefinger. 'Not that I couldn't easily pay my own way,' she says, 'but why buy a dog if you're going to bark yourself?' The shrieky laugh, Dinah notices, has not modified over the decades. 'I haven't brought my plastic, by the way, so I hope you're planning on treating me?'

'Yes, of course,' Dinah says. She wonders, as they proceed to the restaurant, what Michelle has done with the Sugar-Daddy, but she doesn't have to wait for long. Michelle has left him to count out his miscellany of pills in his expensive hotel room in Piccadilly.

'I'm sick of his moaning and snuffling,' Michelle says. 'So I told him I was taking a break.'

In the restaurant, she watches Michelle make a nuisance of herself with the waiters. She demands a run of items that don't appear on the menu and sends back her rack of lamb for various culinary modifications.

'So,' she says, girl-to-girl, when they finally get to the pudding – the pudding for which she requires a specially concocted, syrupy glaze. 'These old roots, eh? Tell me honestly now, Dinah – when you and I were at school together – what did you think of me?'

'Oh,' Dinah says. 'Oh gosh, Michelle—' She does not say that she thought of Michelle hardly at all, or that if she did, it was as a fairly brainless girl with a shrieky laugh. 'I thought you had beautiful hair,' she says. 'I remember that your drawings were very good. I thought you were very sophisticated because you always had that boyfriend.'

Michelle rewards her with an extra loud shriek that causes heads to turn in the restaurant. 'Now I'll tell you what I thought of you,' she says.

'Er—' Dinah says. 'Um—'

'You were a scream,' Michelle says. 'With that hair of yours and the big feet and everything. Gawky. That's what I'd call it. You and that gawky friend as well. I can't remember her name.' Dinah puts down her fork for a moment to drink in this extraordinary fact; that Michelle can't remember Helena's name. 'And I must admit,' Michelle is saying, 'you haven't changed a bit.'

Dinah swallows the impact of this and gestures for the bill, but by now Michelle is in her stride. She and Lorraine are good *managers*, she says. They know how to invest wisely, so that their money keeps on growing. Plus Michelle has ventured into real estate. 'And speaking of roots, Dinah,' she says. 'Why don't you think about a holiday home? Or come back home for good and bring your hubby with you? I mean why should you live in a dump like this? I do luxury condominiums, by the way. And interiors are really my thing. I'm just crazy about Art Deco right now. It's what I'm into, the Deco.'

'Ah,' Dinah says. She turns aside to calculate the gratuity on the Visa slip which the waiter has placed before her. The bill is fifty-nine pounds. She's beginning to feel distinctly rattled. 'It's clever of you to be so good with money,' Dinah says. She's trying to level out the edge in her voice. 'Ours has always burned holes in our pockets,' she says.

She sees Michelle cast a disparaging eye, not only over her newly bobbed hair, but over the Annabel Harrison dress. 'Well, frankly, going by the look of you,' Michelle says, 'I wouldn't say you were one of this life's great spenders.'

Dinah drops Michelle back at the railway station.

'Thanks for a nice evening,' Michelle says. 'I've had a really great time.' Dinah glances up at the electronic information board, which is promising that Michelle's train will, mercifully, arrive on time.

'D'you know I thought I'd tell you,' Michelle is saying, 'Lorraine's asked me to go to your studio, but I don't think I'll have the time. She thinks she'd maybe quite like me to scrounge one of your paintings off you.'

'Ah—' Dinah says. 'I'm afraid that's—'

'That's if there's anything that'll go with her dining room,' Michelle says. 'You've seen her dining room, haven't you? It's a sort of—I don't know—would you call it lime-juice green?'

'Ah—' Dinah says again. She's suddenly begun to wonder whether she's fallen sucker to an episode of *Watch Out. Beadle's About.* Any minute now, a television presenter will come leaping out from the ticket collector's booth and tell her that she's been had.

She starts to laugh. Michelle looks suddenly affronted. 'It's not for *me*,' she says. 'You see I'm fussy about my pictures.'

When Dinah eventually gets home, she finds that her family has retired to bed. She pulls off her shoes and tiptoes to the phone where she dials a number from memory. First she dials the code for Italy; then she dials the code for Venice; finally, she dials her best friend's number, though she knows it's very late – and always an hour later in Italy. But Helena Bevilaqua (née

McKinnon) has always been a night owl and Dinah, of course, knows that she lives on her own. Helena is childless and unattached. She gave up men after the architect who'd replaced the architect whose grandfather had been the architect who designed railway stations for Benito Mussolini. She became an architect herself. Then she gave it up to start a small art publishing business which she runs from her apartment on the Campo San Sebastian. She has no flunkies, no condominiums and no Sugar-Daddy. She doesn't have the time. But she has her professional competence and her sense of fun and her view over the Campo. She also has a comfortable sofabed for when she has a guest; the perennial *Magistretti*.

'I've got a story for you,' Dinah says. 'I'm sorry it's so late.' She tells Helena about the cummerbund and the tawny port and the bell under the carpet. She tells her about Michelle's yellow hair and the Sugar-Daddy and the Art Deco investment properties and the demand for a lime-juice green picture for Lorraine to hang on her wall.

'Bloody hell,' Helena says. 'The highbrow and the tart. Is there anybody normal in the world, Di-do-dee? Except for you and me? Wait. I need a cigarette.'

Together, she and Helena work themselves into giggle mode over the ghastliness of school. 'I expect she's on the phone as we speak,' Dinah says. 'She'll be telling Lorraine how dire her evening with me was.'

'She'll be stuck on the train for hours,' Helena says. There'll be 'an electrical fault in the Didcot area'. There always is.'

'She'll have a mobile,' Dinah says.

'Yesterday,' Helena says, 'I paid the dentist a million lira to replace that buggered front tooth.'

'Send her the bill,' Dinah says. 'No, don't. Then she'll know your address.'

'For Godssake, jump on a plane,' Helena says. 'Do it tomorrow. The family won't mind. Stuff the freezer with those Lean Cuisines. Five each per person per meal. That's what freezers are for.

'*I* will,' Dinah says. 'All right, I will.'

'*Sempre diritto*,' Helena says. 'Can you tell that my voice has gone to pot? She was right about that and all.'

The Professional Wedding Attendee

Aoi Matsushima

I stop my Jaguar at the entrance, and toss the key to the parking staff.

The Imperial Hotel. The glass reflects myself dressed in a black Versace suit with white tie. Appropriate for the occasion. Tall, no extra meat on the body. A bit of grey hair on the sides gives the sign of maturity. The tan from the Caribbean cruise is beginning to fade. Not bad, not bad at all. The doorman bows and opens the door for me.

It's a sunny Sunday in October. It's also Tai-an, the luckiest day of the six-day Buddhist calendar. No wonder the lobby is crowded. I take my invitation card out; the white envelope sealed with a golden label. Mr Murakami's name is on it. The proud father of the groom. I check the name of the banquet room on the signboard. There. The Crane Room. The families of Murakami and Kikuchi.

The Crane Room is at the end of the south wing. After the silence of a long corridor, I hear people gathering already.

'Thank you so much for coming.' The young man standing at the reception on 'the guests of the groom' side bows.

'Congratulations on the wedding,' I bow back, and hand my O-Shugi, the wedding present. The envelope is beautifully decorated with golden strings and with my name in calligraphy. Outstanding among others. The amount inside should be outstanding as well; 100,000 yen, cash, in brand-new notes. Average would be 20,000 yen from friends, 50,000 yen from relatives. This is the occasion to show Mr Murakami my 'appreciation' for inviting me to such a personal event. I'll get enough reward anyway. And I'll put the amount on the invoice next time.

Then I sign my name in the visitor's book. I feel sorry for the man behind me, who has to sign his name next to mine. Ordinary people are not good at calligraphy.

'Mr Arashi, your table will be "Turtle".' The young man hands me a small piece of paper with the word 'Turtle'. The animal that lives longer than others. Not bad.

A waitress offers me a glass of wine in the waiting room.

'Oh, Mr Arashi! Welcome.' Mr Murakami finds me first, and approaches me through his guests.

'Congratulations, Mr Murakami,' I bow deeply.

'Oh, sorry for coming all the way to the wedding of my stupid son,' he bows me back.

Of course he doesn't think of his son as stupid. He can be proud of his son, a graduate of Tokyo University, now a banker, who will inherit the 'Murakami empire'. The son has everything Mr Murakami wanted when he started his career as a small factory owner. It's his big day. Look at him, in a brand-new black kimono, constantly wiping off his sweat.

'A big reception,' I flatter him, looking around the crowd.

'I wanted a proper wedding, you know,' he smiles. 'At first, Takeshi even said he wants to get married in Hawaii. I can't understand the trend of getting married overseas. It's not only his day, but also the best day for the whole family.'

I've heard that story over and over for months. He finally persuaded his son to book the Imperial Hotel, and doubled the number of guests that his son had originally planned. He added some guests he wanted to invite.

'Have you met Mr Taguchi? The Secretary-General of the Liberal Party?' he says.

'Not yet.' Yes, that's the reason I came. I tap on my pocket to confirm that I brought my business cards. I follow Mr Murakami through the guests to the end of the room.

The Secretary-General looks smaller than on TV.

'The Secretary-General, this is Mr Arashi, my lawyer,' Mr Murakami introduces me. Then someone calls him. 'Excuse me,' and he leaves.

'Honoured to meet you, the Secretary-General,' I say, and take out my business card.

'Oh, don't be formal,' says the Secretary-General, showing his golden teeth when he laughs. 'It's Mr Murakami's son's wedding. His big day!'

'Ladies and gentlemen, please enter the Crane Room,' the hotel manager calls.

Every one starts to move, and I miss the chance to give him my card. Shit.

The wedding march is played loudly. The door opens, and the couple comes in. Applause. They bow, and walk nervously through the tables to the main long table facing the guests.

I've met Takeshi once a long time ago at Mr Murakami's office. I can't believe that this kid is getting married. And I check the girl in the white wedding dress, every girl's dream. A costume changes even the horse driver (fine feathers make fine birds), it's said.

'Ladies and gentleman, thank you so much for coming to the wedding reception of Takeshi Murakami and Naoko Kikuchi,' the MC, a friend of Takeshi who works at the national television, announces.

'Now, I would like to have a word from Mr Yamada, the matchmaker of the two. Mr Yamada is the director of Kanto Bank which Takeshi is working for.'

Mr Yamada stands up. He and his wife in her black kimono are seated on either side of the wedding couple. He looks nervous.

'Is he Takeshi's boss?' the woman sitting next to me asks her husband.

'No,' he whispers. 'Takeshi first asked his boss, who he works with, to be the matchmaker. But when the boss knew the number of the guests at the party, he passed the role to his boss. And that boss passed it on to his boss, Mr Yamada.'

'I thought the matchmaker was the one who gave the couple a chance to see each other.'

'It is, originally. But he hadn't seen Takeshi nor Naoko till they formally asked him for the matchmaker. It often happens.'

'I am pleased to announce to you,' the instant matchmaker begins, 'that they were married at the church in this hotel two hours ago . . .'

His role is mainly to introduce the couple to the guests. His speech is as boring as most matchmakers' speeches. All the grooms are smart, active, and full of future possibilities. All the brides are beautiful, gentle, and wise.

After the matchmaker's speech we all make a toast, and the waiters start to serve the soup.

The Professional Wedding Attendee

The 'Turtle' table is the best table, in front of the main stage where the newly-wed couple sit: the Secretary-General, the Professor of Tokyo University, the president of the Kanto Bank. I sit next to the wife of the man Mr Murakami works with. I wonder why Mr Murakami put me three seats away from the Secretary-General.

Laughter is heard from other tables; friends and relatives – this is a good occasion for reunion. But no one knows each other on our table, and maybe none of us know the wedding couple well either. What can we talk about – a politician, an economist, an academic, a factory owner, and a housewife?

'Beautiful flowers, aren't they?' I break the uncomfortable silence. Then I turn to the woman next to me. Wise to start with women. 'Do you know the name?'

'*Teoopu-yuri*,' she smiles.

Good. Women like to feel superior to men knowing these tiny things. Well, the flower arrangement is not bad. I guess it is the second from the best, from the list of the flower arrangements the hotel provides. It's very Mr Murakami, to choose the second, to save money with these small things.

I ignore the sound the Secretary-General makes when he sips the soup.

Speeches. That's the boring part of the reception. The speechmakers take turns, from Takeshi's side, then the girl's. There are so many words you are not allowed to say. Cut, break, divide, split . . . not appropriate for the wedding. I'm glad that I'm not making one this time.

The Secretary-General makes the first speech, as the main guest. But what can he say to the couple he's never met? He congratulates them, gives them general advice on how to keep the relationship going.

His best joke is: 'The population of Japan is declining. I hope you will have children, at least two, very soon.'

I try to clap and laugh loud, so that he will be pleased. A cliché, but a good try.

After him, this line becomes fashionable among all the other speakers.

'As the Secretary-General said earlier, I hope she will have many children. He said two, but I think three is a good number.'

'I do agree with the Secretary-General, so I wish them to have many children as well – three, maybe four would be better.'

The number of children increases as the speeches go on.

'Now, please excuse the bride for a while for her "Colour-Maintenance",' the MC announces. The colour maintenance means changing her dress. That's one of the attractions of weddings.

'I've heard that Naoko wanted to keep her wedding dress on all through the reception,' says the woman next to me. 'But her mother insisted that it was her dream to see her daughter in the kimono which she wore at her own wedding. Then, you know what? Takeshi's mother offered to buy her a beautiful pink evening dress from France. Battle of mothers. Naoko was wise enough not to upset her future mother-in-law. So she changes twice.'

Oh, I shouldn't have given her the chance to gossip with me.

While Naoko is changing her dress, we can relax, eat and talk.

Mr Murakami comes all the way from his family table

The Professional Wedding Attendee

at the end, to the main table, to thank the Secretary-General, offering him a glass of beer. Great opportunity!

'I'll take a photo of you two!' I say, taking a small camera from my pocket. The smallest camera, the latest model.

'That's a good idea!' Mr Murakami says. 'Why don't you join us, Mr Suzuki? Come on, Mr Maeda . . .'

Well, a huge group photo is not to my taste, but it's fine, as long as I can get a chance to send the Secretary-General this photo later.

The trend of wedding receptions has become quieter in the '90s. But there are some attractions still remaining. Cutting the cake is the main one. Of course, Mr Murakami has arranged a huge, three-storied fake cake. The idea of small real cakes has been rejected.

'This is the most memorable moment of their lives,' the MC says, 'Those who have cameras, please come closer to the main stage to take photos!'

'Why don't you go?' the gossipy woman says to me. 'I know you are hiding a tiny camera in your pocket!'

Can anyone shut this bitch up? I'm not a photographer.

Later in the ceremony, it's time for the friends of the couple to make speeches. Usually the groom is betrayed by the things he has done at school. Stupid.

Then the bride's girlfriends sing a love song. The girl in the black short dress has good legs. Looks better than the others.

'What's the title of this song?' the Secretary-General asks.

' "Samba of the Ladybird",' I reply in a second.

'Oh, you know youth culture very well, don't you?' He is impressed.

I won't say that the song was a hit twenty years ago.

When Naoko returns from her second dress change, they do the candle service. Another attraction. They walk through the tables to light the candles with the long candle they carry. Takes ages to arrive at the main table. Waste of time. I check my Rolex.

The final event. At last. It is, of course, the flower giving to their parents. Naoko's parents are rather embarrassed under the spotlights, but Mr Murakami looks happy. It is his big day.

Takeshi gives a big bouquet to Naoko's mother, and Naoko gives another one to Takeshi's mother. Takeshi's mother's crying.

'She doesn't want her son to leave their house,' the gossipy bitch says. 'She's not an easy mother-in-law.'

At the end of the ceremony, Mr Murakami makes a speech to thank all the guests for coming. 'This couple are still very young,' he says, the conventionally-worded address. 'But please support them as they start their new life.'

This man is very creative.

Sigh of relief. The reception is over, finally. People start to move.

I notice that the Secretary-General forgets to take the big paper bag, the gift for the guests, which the hotel staff has set underneath the chair.

I dash to his chair, take it out, and hand it to him.

'Oh, that's very kind of you,' he says. 'What was your name again?'

'Arashi. The storm.'

'Yes, thank you, Mr Storm.'

Yes. I finally succeed in making him remember my

name. Good. And to make sure, I slip my business card into his paper bag. Smart move.

Well, this three-hour reception was not completely a waste of time.

I take my paper bag from under my chair. It is as big as a shopping bag, and heavier than usual. Maybe a set of porcelain from Mr Murakami's home town. And a piece of wedding cake, a box of chocolates. I'll put most of them straight into my closet.

The couple and the parents thank me at the exit. That's my last bow for today.

I walk through the young people, the friends taking pictures. They are going to the casual 'Second Party' at the restaurant nearby.

I don't have to go.

I walk out of the hotel, and the fresh air feels good.

Why do people bother to get married? A living hell, it is always said. Who still believes in the love of a lifetime?

I give my ticket to the parking attendant, and wait for my Jaguar.

I glance at the entrance, and see the girl in the black dress coming out alone. She looks at the long queue for a taxi. And she notices me, gently bows.

'Nice wedding, wasn't it?' I say, casually.

'Yes, indeed,' she replies, but sounds cynical.

'Too formal, maybe.' I change my tone, according to hers.

'It was a big reception. I am a bit tired.'

'Aren't you going to the "Second Party"?'

'No, I am too tired, and I don't know her friends from school. I'm her colleague.'

'So, you are working at the bank?'

'Yes, I am.'

Good. The girls working at the banks are wealthy.

'A long queue for the taxi, isn't it?'

'Yes, I'll walk to the station, to take the subway.'

'It must be hard to walk with the pin-heel,' I said. Women like delicate and sensitive comments.

'Well, yes, but...'

'Would you like a lift?'

'Oh, no, I'm all right.'

My Jaguar arrives just on time. The attendant returns my key.

'Oh, is that your car?' the girl says, with admiration.

'Yes, maybe faster than a subway. Hop in!'

'But...'

'Which station is convenient for you?'

Girls can't resist my offer. She's too tired, and probably I look more mature than anyone she has met.

It's been a long day. I deserve a short break.

Deptford Girls

Kate Mosse

> The bos'n pipes the watch below,
> Yen ho! lads! ho!
> Then here's a health afore we go.
> A long, long life to my sweet wife an' mates at sea;
> An' keep our bones from Davy Jones, where'er we be.
>
> From the ballad 'Nancy Lee' performed aboard the *Princess Alice*, September 1878

The traffic on the Broadway invariably bottlenecked on Wednesdays when the High Street shut. All the heavy lorries on their way to Dover. All the salesmen in their clean company cars, jackets hanging from the hooks in the back, tapping their fingers on the steering wheel. Impatient, hating to be forced to wait and each desperate to get away first. To get the advantage.

Sarah waited and watched as the other lines of traffic drew to a halt. For a couple of seconds nobody moved, then the main lights turned green and the front runners surged out of the gates, off up the hill towards Blackheath.

The roar of the Broadway always came as a surprise after the calm of the back streets. From her flat, she'd gone up Brookmill Road to the bottom of St John's Vale, where the smell of stale beer seeped out from the pub on the corner and floated in the damp October air. The cellarman clanked and rolled his empty barrels into the waiting lorry. He was early, for once. Along Cranbrook Road, avoiding the dogshit and pensioners heading for the sub-post office. Over Friendly Street and down through the white clapboard estate towards Tanner's Hill and Wellbeloved the Butcher, then onto the Broadway.

Sarah held her breath, trying not to inhale the diesel and petrol fumes. The whine of their engines grew fainter. None of them, she was sure, had paid the slightest attention to the small streets they'd been driving through. The booze shops hidden behind metal grilles, the burger joint and 24-hour supermarket where the drunks congregated like gatecrashers at a wedding, trying to make friends with anyone who made eye contact.

Sarah tried to imagine her landscape as outsiders might see it and knew it would look tatty and depressing and poor. Of no account. They wouldn't see the stories beneath the cobbles nor the character of this dirty old bit of town. She wondered, sometimes, at this affection she felt for Deptford, her obsession with the place. What did it say about her that she felt so at home in this part of London? Her parents would dismiss it as inverted snobbery. Or, if they were feeling charitable, put it down to an ability – it goes without saying, inherited – to make do? Actually, though, it was simple. She felt she belonged. And with no job, no significant others, a few fractured friendships, she had little else to fill her thoughts or her days.

Sarah crossed to Deptford High Street, paved these days in pretty grey bricks that were hopeless for wheelchairs or pushchairs. A piece of urban art – what town planners and the *Daily Mail* call a 'feature' – a large black wrought-iron anchor set in stone, reminded shoppers of Deptford's maritime past. Kids were clambering over it, hooking their legs over the arms and hanging upside down like monkeys. The hoods of their cheap coats flopped over their faces and muffled their giggles.

Although it was only 9.15, the market was already in full swing. Men shouting into microphones, selling toasters, dinner sets, sofas. You want it, they'd got it. Sarah negotiated her way along the crowded aisle between the two rows of stalls, their red and white plastic awnings rustling and flapping in the wind.

This was not the part of the market that interested her. Gaudy towels, cheap shoes, CDs, and someone selling Jesus. She had statues, Bibles, embroidered pictures with Christ's face stitched in bright gold thread on shiny black material, like a pauper's Turin Shroud. Gospel music proclaimed the happy day and a man, half-preaching, half-singing, welcomed in the lost and the found.

And it was clearly working because the stall was full, mainly with women, their shopping trolleys parked behind them in a line. As they thumbed the prayers and dedications, they talked of the price of air fares to Jamaica and just how reasonable was the price of faith these days? Only fifty pence a prayer or three for a pound. A bargain.

Sarah ducked to avoid the halal meat hanging out over the pavement and tried not to catch the bulging eye of the red snapper and hake and salt fish in their white crates outside the fishmonger. If she looked up, above the hustle of the market, she could see the restored curve of the Regency houses above the shops which sold no-questions-asked insurance or advertised fail-safe, secure methods of sending money back home. The bricks were pale now, faded from their glory days when the docks and the Empire thrived and Deptford was a place with prospects. Higher still, there was a prisoner's sky. A square patch of blue, surrounded by grimy, drizzled clouds. Beneath her feet, blood leaked from the fish and meat down into the gutter.

At the corner, Sarah turned left towards the Albany and the area of the market where the traders shifted their house clearances. History for sale, wholesale. When there was nobody left in a family, entire lives could end up down here in Deptford Market. Precious ornaments, Sunday Best, photographs, all flogged off to pay for the coffin. She walked fast, knowing the crowds would start to build up. Past the fruit and veg, the outsized thermal underwear, the Chinese convenience store and the vacuum cleaner parts, and into the square itself.

The rest of the week, boys on blades and undersized bikes spun and jumped and twisted their wheels in shows of bravado and risk. On Wednesdays, the square looked like a jumble sale.

Sarah stopped for a moment, feeling that bubble of excitement familiar to all charity shop girls. That, today, she would find a jewel amongst all the rubbish. A bit of treasure. Furniture, clothes, bicycles, puzzles. Mountains of clothes and shoes piled high on green tarpaulins stretched out on the ground. The smell of age and decay was worse on wet mornings, like a compost of lives lived and forgotten. The musty smell reminded her of old houses, the scent mingling with the sizzle of fried sausages and onions and roasted coffee from the breakfast van in the corner.

To her right, a huge boarded table, like a stage, took up most of one side of the square. Every inch was covered with junk and, in the middle, a woman with a lined, suspicious face sat perched on an iron stool, watching the many hands fingering her wares, picking things up, putting things down, checking for damage or brand names. A Barbie with no hair, a pair of horseshoe bookends, a frosted glass vase, brass hooks, pirate videos claiming to be ex-rental. Sold as seen, no guarantees. Buyer beware.

The scrabblers held things up and waited for Dee to catch their eye. She never engaged in conversation, just snapped the price. Quid, one-fifty, six for a quid. No negotiation. Like a ringmaster in a circus, she remained alert to the possibility that the animals circling could turn on her.

Sarah wasn't in the mood for Dee, so headed for one of the traders in the middle of the square. His quality books were displayed on spinners and in rows on a table, but he'd tipped the rest onto an old red curtain spread on the ground. They might not be worth much, but there was no point letting the mould get into them.

'Ten for a pound, love.'

Sarah nodded, although she knew anyway.

In the past, she'd picked up a faded leather-bound 1904 edition of *Bleak House*, armfuls of Agatha Christies, Ngaio Marshes and Gladys Mitchells and a few classics that she'd still not got round to reading. Sarah squatted down and started systematically to work the piles, focused and methodical as she moved books from place to place, careful not to miss anything. If a book spiked her interest, she checked that the pages weren't stuck together or missing or that bits of food or worse weren't pressed between its covers. If it got a clean bill of health, she'd put it with the 'definites' or the 'maybes'.

Ten hand-picked books every Wednesday. Too busy reading about other people's lives to have one of your own, her mother said.

Perhaps there were more books than usual or just more 'maybes', but Sarah went into her book trance, as a friend once put it. She lost track now, of her surroundings and of the day changing around her. She didn't hear the rumbling in the sky, didn't notice how the drizzle had turned to rain or how the awnings pegged over the tables were snagged and twitched by the wind.

'You done, love?'

She peered up. 'Sorry?'

'It's gonna chuck it down any minute now. I gotta get this lot covered up.'

'Sorry,' she said. 'I'll take these.'

'You got ten there?'

He was in too much of a hurry to want to count.

'Ten, yes.'

'That'll be a quid then, love. Need a bag?'

A few minutes later, Sarah was sitting in Revival Café on the High Street, hands cupped round a hot mug. The plate-glass windows were already steamed up, the consequence of too many people in too little space. Outside, clouds of umbrellas jostled in the High Street, black and red and white and blue as people rushed for shelter. The traders had thrown bin liners over their stock, hoping the storm would pass quickly and let them get back to earning a living.

The queue at the till grew longer as more people splattered in, stamping their dripping feet on the mat and shaking umbrellas out the door. A little girl was writing her name on the window with her finger.

Sarah checked her watch: 9.50. Usually, she read the paper, the free locals, had her breakfast, took it easy. Usually, she saved her shopping – her 'new' books – until she got home. After all, it helped the time to pass. But since she hadn't paid attention to the last three books she'd grabbed as the rain began, Sarah stuck her hand into the carrier bag and pulled out what was on the top of the pile.

It wasn't a book at all. It was a diary or rather a record of events, a journal. Thin spidery writing, a few dates, all cramped up as if the writer didn't think she'd ever have enough paper to finish.

This is the private property of Miss Alice Sarah Livett of 12 Albury Street, Deptford, S.E. If lost please return to rightful owner.

The back pages were filled with columns, Sarah guessed the weekly housekeeping accounts of everything required in Albury Street. Cloth, firewood, coal, horsemeat, wax, rum. She had to screw up her eyes to decipher the tiny letters. Next to each entry, a record of the cost.

At the beginning of the book was a list of birthdays and important events, all written in a formal fashion. Different colours of ink and subtle changes in the handwriting gave the impression that the list had been built up over many years.

15th May 1870. Robert William Livett to Isobel Grace Harris. Married St Paul's Church, Deptford.
18th June, 1871. Florence Isobel. Born Evelyn Street.
20th June, 1873. Nancy Grace. Born Evelyn Street.
24th May, 1874. Hilda Eugenie. Born Evelyn Street.
17th February, 1878. Alice Sarah. Born Albury Street.
3rd September, 1878. Princess Alice.
19th September 1903. R W Livett to Mary Chalker. Married St Paul's Church, Deptford.
20th May 1904. Grace Charlotte. Born Albury Street.

The list of dates filled several pages. It seemed to

contain few references to anything outside Alice's immediate circle of family and neighbours and royalty. Years of day trips, visits to and from Albury Street, local events were all here. The death of Queen Victoria was recorded, as was the Jubilee of King George V in 1935, but most national and world events went unremarked. Even the First and Second World Wars did not appear and the final entry was strangely inconsequential.

25th November, 1944. Woolworth's with G.

It was an unsatisfying finale. Sarah flipped through and checked to see if pages had been torn out. But there was no entry in the diary itself to explain why Alice suddenly had stopped writing.

Sarah glanced at the counter, hoping the queue had died down and she could get another coffee to keep her going. She didn't want to be forced to stop reading and give up her table. To establish her credentials, she even bought a sandwich and spread herself out more to make sure nobody joined her.

By skimming backwards and forwards between the dates at the front and the diary entries themselves, little by little Sarah began to build up a picture of Alice's life. She appeared to have been brought up by her father alone. Despite the evidence of three older sisters, none of them were mentioned in the journal. At the age of fourteen, Alice was apprenticed to a local dressmaker, but continued living in Albury Street with her father and remained there when he remarried in 1903.

Sarah frowned, surprised by the fact that no explanation was given in the diary for the absence of Alice's mother and sisters. There were no more than a handful of references to the second Mrs Livett and the care of Grace, the child of that remarriage, seemed to have fallen to Alice.

But Sarah liked reading about streets she recognised.

It made Alice seem a friend. She could imagine the route Alice walked to work, could picture the tram lines and the big shops in Lewisham and New Cross. Could picture the gentle, confined pace of Alice's life lived in and around Deptford. Neither Alice nor her younger half-sister Grace ever married, but both were clearly regular churchgoers and members of various Bible Groups who met in the Wesleyan Hall round the back of Sayes Court. Certain days stood out. For example, a day trip with local schoolchildren to the seaside in 1925. Not Margate or Southend, but up river to the mudflats by Tower Bridge to make mud-and-sand pies in the sunshine.

After a long illness, Alice's father had died in 1926. And there, in Alice's diary entry for his last few days, was the record of a conversation between father and daughter. Sarah cross-checked with the list of dates and, sure enough, found the entry she wanted. *3rd September, 1878. Princess Alice.*

Sarah had thought the reference odd when she'd read it in the calendar. The entry somehow didn't fit in, listed as it was in the middle of the Livett family birthdays. So, she'd carried on reading and thought no more about it. Now, nosey or curious, Sarah wanted to know. After all, she had nothing else to do. If Alice wouldn't explain, then the library should. It would take care of the rest of the morning, if nothing else.

The screen flickered as Sarah read.

On Tuesday 3rd September, 1878, the London Steamship Company's pleasure paddle steamer, the *Princess Alice*, sailed on a day trip to Gravesend and Sheerness. Among the 700 passengers were a Mrs Hawks, the owner of the Anchor and Hope pub at Charlton, a group of 'ladies of the night' from the Seven Dials area of

London, forty women from Smithfield's Cowcross Mission, and a group from a Bible class which included Mrs Isobel Livett and her three daughters, Florence, Nancy and Hilda, aged seven, five and four respectively. A younger daughter had been left at home with her father.

It was 8.45 in the evening as the steamer approached Gallions Reach. Many of the passengers, in good spirits from their day out, were below deck in the restaurant bar listening to the live entertainment provided by Mr Maybrick. Accompanied by a ramshackle choir made up of the steamer's crew, he was performing the ballad 'Nancy Lee'.

As the steamer rounded the bend between Crossness and Margaret Ness near Tripcock Point, she met the steam collier, *Bywell Castle*, which had just off-loaded her cargo at Millwall Dock and was returning to the South Shore. The collier ploughed into the *Princess Alice*, splitting her down the middle. The stern and bows folded upwards and, within minutes, the ship had gone down, taking almost everyone with her. Victorian ladies, mostly unable to swim, were pulled down by their crinolines and skirts. Few made it to the shore, even though it was only 300 yards away. Others died choking on pollution from the Southern Outfall Works as the ebb tide swept them towards Erith. A police officer pulled his wife from the water, then went back for the ship's flag. When he returned to shore he found the woman he had saved was a stranger and his wife was drowned. He later married the stranger.

The bodies brought ashore were taken mainly to Woolwich Dockyard and Roff's Wharf and numbered if their names were not known. Some drifted as far as Gravesend, where they were laid for claiming in the pier waiting room. On 21st September, the *Kentish Mercury* printed a list of those whose remains had been identified.

A large Celtic cross was raised at Woolwich Cemetery by public subscription, 23,000 people giving sixpence each to make a grave for the 160 unclaimed victims.

Captain Grinsted, the experienced and respected master of the *Princess Alice*, died along with his fourteen-year-old son, a cabin boy. His name was misspelled in most reports and on his death certificate. It was no surprise that Grinstead Road, off Evelyn Street, which was named after him, was also spelled wrongly.

The *Princess Alice* was new in 1865. It was originally licensed to carry 486 passengers, but this was increased to 936 in 1878 after a refit. The Board of Trade considered one lifeboat and one longboat to provide adequate safety precautions, despite the fact they could embark no more than sixty people apiece. Coincidentally, Princess Alice herself, after whom the steamer was named, died three months later.

Someone, nearby, coughed and Sarah realised she'd been longer than she intended. Removing the microfiche from the reader, she gathered her belongings at the terminal, then checked herself out at the desk.

From the library she turned right, back onto Giffin Street, picking her way around the puddles. Past the haberdashery stall, past the shoes, then across the High Street, back to the books again.

After all, it is always more interesting – easier – to live in other people's lives.

The Iron Claw

Marion Mathieu

It was Saturday and the factory had shipped the big order out on Thursday, so Dad didn't have to get up at four a.m. and drive all the way into the city to open up. He hardly ever got a weekend off, so I was glad he was getting some rest, but Mom's idea of a treat was not cooking breakfast till we could all 'sit down together as a family', even though it was nearly eleven and Peggy and me were starving to death. We opened his door a crack and whispered *Daddy*, but he just kept on sleeping in that weird way he had, with his eyes staring up at the ceiling and shuddery sounds coming from the back of his throat.

A big sneeze finally woke him, and he rolled over and screwed his face up like he didn't know who we were. Then he hunted around on the floor for one of his old *Popular Mechanics*, took it into the toilet and stayed there till he must have read it three or four times over. But at least Mom counted that as 'up' and she tied on her apron and told Peggy and me to start setting the table.

We were picking bits of milk bottle off the floor when Dad finally made it to the kitchen, beating his hands on his chest and doing Tarzan yells. He had pyjama bottoms on but no slippers, so Mom said *Watch it!* and waved a spatula at the broken glass. Dad hollered, *You, Jane!*

grabbed Mom round the waist and pretended to take a big bite out of her neck. She flipped the eggs and told him to put some clothes on, but her mouth was curving upwards and her cheeks were bright red.

His right hand went all stiff and shaky then, like it wasn't part of his body anymore, and he looked real scared and shouted, 'Run for your lives – it's the Iron Claw!' The sausages were turning black, so Mom jabbed him with her elbow and yanked the frying pan off the burner, but Peggy and me ran, and the evil hand with Dad stuck behind it chased us all around the house. It was so scary I stopped looking back, but I could still hear this deep spooky voice going, 'The... Iron... Claw' over and over again.

We got to our bedroom and Peggy slammed the door, but the hand started banging and pounding and trying to get in. I felt like throwing up, even though I knew it was Dad on the other side, and Peggy's face went dead white except for two bits of purple under her eyes. She put her shoulder and I put my back against the door, and we screamed and pushed as hard as we could. All the time the doorknob was rattling and the hinges were shaking and that creepy voice kept moaning, 'You can't escape... from the *Iron Claw*.'

Then everything went quiet, so I pushed Peggy out of the way, opened the door a crack and peeked through. Dad had changed into his good suit and was fiddling around with a big silver camera. I glanced back at Peggy, but there was a net curtain on her head and she'd put on a clunky white dress that looked like Grandma's Sunday tablecloth with the gravy stains washed out. She hadn't said anything about playing bride and I was all set to tell her there was no way I was being groom, when I looked down and saw that somebody had stitched me into a tablecloth too.

Dad whistled and said *How's my girls?* and took us into the kitchen. Mom had curled her hair, swept up the rest of the glass, and buttoned herself into a shiny grey dress I'd never seen her in before. There was no sign of eggs or sausages so I figured breakfast must have gone straight into the bin, but there was a lopsided cake with lots of drippy white icing on the table.

I felt like stuffing the whole thing in my mouth, even though I knew it would be dry on top and squishy at the bottom, but Mom was in no hurry to cut it. She told Peggy and me to stand side by side and press our hands together like we were praying, so Dad could get some nice pictures. I tried to keep my eyes open and look holy, but it wasn't easy with flashbulbs going off in my face.

Mom said that Peggy and me had really stood out in the procession and hadn't been overdressed like some of those little Italian girls. I elbowed Peggy and whispered, *WHAT procession?* but she shushed me and kept looking holy even though Dad had already put the camera away.

I was just getting up the nerve to ask for a piece of cake when I looked over and saw it was gone. So was my dress and Peggy and me were back in shorts, only her face looked skinny and we were taller than we'd ever been in Mom's high heels. I smelled peanut butter, but Peggy beat me to the table, twisted the cap back on the jar, and said I could at least start stacking the plates.

Mom had changed into pedal pushers and stuck her head in the sink. I told her I was hungry, but she said I shouldn't have been so picky at lunch. She stuck a towel on her head and went outside. Dad got two beers from the fridge and followed her. Peggy and me threw the dirty dishes in the sink and ran over to the window to watch.

Mom was sitting on the picnic bench with her head

ducked down, running her fingers through her hair and shaking it dry in the sun. Dad pressed a bottle against her arm and she jumped, then he stuck two cigarettes into his mouth and lit them. Mom pushed her hair out of her face and took a cigarette and a beer. She crossed her legs and waved the cigarette around more than she smoked it. Every now and then she'd clink bottles with Dad and take a big long swallow of beer. They came back in laughing about what a rough week they'd had and how they could really use a nap. Peggy and me made a start on the dishes, but they said we should go out and get some fresh air.

The Jehovah's Witness boy from next door had stretched too, but still had dark wavy hair and long eyelashes. He slammed his book shut and ran inside as soon as he saw us. Peggy stopped me from calling him back. She said the last thing we needed was some weirdo who never said the school prayer and wouldn't even stand up for the Pledge of Allegiance.

Peggy and me weren't too good at thinking up games. All we ever did was stand on either side of the septic tank and bounce a ball back and forth. I could see the Jehovah's Witness boy watching from his bedroom, so I started laughing like I was having some really great time. Peggy told me to stop acting like a jerk, that I could go off and *be* a Jehovah's Witness for all she cared, but not to come crying to her when I didn't get any Christmas or birthday presents.

She said I couldn't have transfusions, even if a tree fell on me and I was bleeding to death. I kept looking up at the Jehovah's Witness boy's window and wondering if my new long legs had scared him, since we'd been playing in his room just the day before. There was a picture in his Bible I'd really liked of a boy and girl sitting on the back of a lion, but he'd said that was *his* Heaven and Catholics weren't allowed in.

It was Peggy's turn to bounce the ball, but she hung onto it and skipped back to the house. The side door was open and Dad was helping Mom down the steps. She had a fat stomach and a hot puffy face, but he said she'd be okay soon and to go inside and not give our grandmother any trouble.

Peggy and me asked if we could play Pick-Up Sticks in our room, but Grandma told us to sit on the sofa where she could keep an eye on us. She was hogging the whole paper, so I asked for the comics, and she got really mad when I explained it was in four sections that Mom and Dad always divided up between us. My stomach was rumbling, so I asked if we could heat up some macaroni and cheese, but she just made an annoyed sound in her throat and kept smoking and coughing and reading obituaries out loud.

Then the phone rang, and she came back wiping her eyes with the same handkerchief she'd been coughing into. She said that we should bow our heads and say a prayer for our baby brother, 'cause his soul had been so pure, God couldn't wait to have it by His side. I asked if that meant old people were the souls God wasn't in any big hurry for, and she gave me a whack on the side of my head.

Mom came back skinny in a dress that had loops round the waist but no belt. Before she could even sit down Grandma was going *Thank God* there'd been a priest there, so at least they'd have the comfort of knowing poor little Patrick Daniel wasn't stuck in Limbo with all those unbaptised babies who could never look upon the face of God. Dad gave her a dirty look and rattled the car keys but Grandma said *Never you mind*, she'd be perfectly all right on the bus.

Mom put the kettle on and asked her to at least stay for a cup of tea, but Grandma told Peggy and me to get her suitcase, and made a big show of not letting Dad help with her coat. She tried to slam the door behind her but it got stuck on the mat, so she banged it with her handbag and muttered *Jesus, Mary and Joseph* instead.

Mom decided to be alone in the bedroom for a while. Dad yawned and stretched out on the sofa, and Peggy and me climbed into the easy chair to watch him. His eyes were moving under the lids, and his face and hands kept twitching, almost like a sleeping cat. I laughed and said he was having Iron Claw dreams, but Peggy said that was baby stuff only a dopey kid like me would even remember.

Then Mom came back and whispered, 'He's been working very hard,' like we were too stupid to figure that out for ourselves, but she offered to make fried egg sandwiches so I forgave her. I tried to get up, but Peggy's hip was digging into mine, our bottoms were wedged into the cushions, and my shorts felt so tight I figured Mom must have shrunk them in the wash.

Mom was pretty strong for someone who'd just sent a baby to Heaven. She grabbed Peggy's right arm and my left, and pulled us both out in one go. I was wondering when she'd managed to get her hair cut short when I noticed that Peggy's had grown halfway down her back and was shinier that I'd ever seen it.

Mom cooked the eggs till they were black on the bottom and rubbery on top. Then she pushed over a shiny-paged little book called *Growing Up*. Peggy tilted her chair away from the table and started fiddling with her hair, but I peeked at a few of the pictures, which were mostly outlines of girls with lima beans growing inside them. Mom took a deep breath, muttered *This is more than anybody ever told me*, and kept on talking till our sandwiches had gone greasy and cold.

It was mostly about Italian boys and how most of them were shaving by the time they were thirteen. If we weren't careful we'd get pregnant and Dad would have to fork out for big noisy weddings and we'd wind up stuck in our in-laws' basements cooking spaghetti every night.

There was a big crash then. Mom, Peggy and me jumped up from the table, Dad rolled off the sofa, and we all ran outside. Somebody had chopped down the woods and stuck three new houses across the street. Our driveway was full of people I'd never seen before, all waving their arms and shouting in Italian, and there was a pointy black car where our mailbox used to be. Dad's lips went tight, but when he saw they were pulling a fat little girl out of the driver's seat he put on his 'take charge' voice and kept saying, 'Is she okay? That's all that matters. Is she okay?'

She was called Baby Tina, and she'd climbed into the car and released the handbrake while the rest of the family had been sitting in the garage eating lunch. Mr Petraglia pumped Dad's hand up and down and promised to pay for everything. Mrs Petraglia kept pointing at Mom, Peggy, and me, and going, 'So slim... so young... and with two big girls,' so Mom made her mouth smile and said, 'Oh, you can't take your eyes off them for a *second*.'

Rudy Petraglia had slicked-back hair, tight shiny pants, and high-heeled boots with zippers up the side. He offered to show Peggy and me the house. I wondered why a teenager was bothering to talk to us, but then I saw that Peggy had breasts and when I looked down I had them too.

Rudy took us around the back way so nobody would

see us going in. He showed us a dining-room with big glass cabinets and a chandelier, but said they ate most of their meals off a picnic table in the garage. They didn't use the living-room much either. The lampshades were wrapped in cellophane, there were plastic runners on the carpet, and the sofa crackled when I sat down.

Rudy caught me looking at a bumpy orange painting of a bullfighter. He stamped his feet and waved an imaginary cape. Peggy laughed like he was funniest thing she'd ever seen, so he twirled her around till she was dizzy and told her about all the great records they could dance to up in his room.

I told Peggy I'd wait. My stomach was rumbling and even a cold fried egg would have tasted pretty good, but I figured Mom had fed the sandwiches to the birds by now. There was a bowl of fruit next to me. I tried to peel a banana, but it had a hole poked in its bottom and a waxy seam running down one side. Then I felt sort of queasy and damp between my legs, so I ran back across the street to tell Mom I'd got one of those periods she'd been warning us about.

We had a new mailbox, but I only half-noticed it. All the good stuff was going on next door. There was a sofa with a big black hole in it on Mr Laverty's front lawn, the old man was curled up in the weeds next to it, and Dad was soaking them both down with the garden hose. I heard a siren, then a long red truck came flashing round the corner. A load of firemen thumped into the house while the chief prodded Mr Laverty with his boot and told him he was lucky to have such a quick-thinking neighbour.

Mr Laverty looked up, coughed and passed out again. The chief made a speech about the dangers of drinking, smoking, and falling asleep. Dad asked if he could give the old boy another blast of the hose, to pay him back for all those times he'd woken us at four in the morning singing 'That Lil' Ol' Wine Drinker, Me'.

Then Mom pulled up in a noisy yellow car and nearly took the mailbox down again. Her face was so pale Dad forgot all about hosing Mr Laverty and took her straight into the house instead. I sneaked into the bathroom, rinsed out my knickers, and changed into clean ones with half a roll of toilet paper stuffed inside.

I was dying to ask where the sanitary pads were hidden and when Mom had learned to drive, but she was shivering on the sofa, telling Dad how her brain had forgotten to tell her foot to brake for a red light. A young traffic cop had pulled her over and asked to see some identification, but she'd pushed open the door and rolled out on the pavement instead. He'd just laughed and said, 'I think you'd better go *home*, lady.'

Mom said her feet and hands were like ice, so Dad cranked the heat up as far as it would go and told me to pull the quilt off their bed. By the time I got back she was burning up. Dad said if he kept messing around with the thermostat it'd break, and weren't there pills or something she could take.

I put the quilt down on the sofa. When I looked back up, Mom's hair was salt and pepper and Dad's had gone white over the ears. One of them was bound to ask where Peggy was, so I was relieved when she came banging back through the front door. She looked sort of like Mom had that morning, only rounder, and had a baby in a pushchair and two little boys hanging onto her skirt.

There was a shiny new mirror next to the door. I peeked into it and saw a skinnier version of Mom. Peggy made a crack about how I'd better get some meat on my bones if I wanted Rudy's friend Sal to take me to the Demolition Derby Saturday night. I nodded and had a look at the gold-framed wedding photo on the wall. Rudy looked scared, but Peggy was grinning and holding an enormous bouquet over her stomach.

Mom wandered into the kitchen, sighing, 'Well, I guess you're all hungry,' opened a can of tomato soup and started squirting Cheese Whiz on Ritz crackers. I tried to steal one, but she slapped my hand away and said to stop acting like a greedy little kid. Then I remembered my period. The toilet paper must have fallen out of my knickers, but I felt dry down there anyway, so I figured I'd wait till next month to tell her.

Grandma was sitting at the kitchen table. She called over Rudy Junior, gave him a nickel, and told him he had lovely blue eyes, just like his Great-Grandad in Heaven. Then she said in a really loud voice what a blessing it was at least *one* of them looked a *bit* like *our* side of the family.

Little Tony had brown eyes and dark skin. He asked if he could have a nickel too, but Grandma just ignored him. Peggy found one in her handbag and gave it to him. She told him he looked just like his handsome daddy, then made her voice even louder than Grandma's and said that Rudy was getting lots of overtime in the auto body shop, so they'd be moving out of the Petraglias' basement real soon.

I was waiting for Grandma to answer back, but she'd gone real quiet. Then her head dropped forward and her teeth fell out. Rudy Junior let out a shriek and did a funny little hopping dance, Mom shouted into the phone for an ambulance, and Dad set Grandma down on the floor with a chair cushion under her head. Peggy put her arms around Rudy Junior and told him the ambulance men would make it okay, but I could see Grandma was as dead as a doornail, so I went into my room, closed the door, and got into bed.

It was dark when I woke up. I went back into the living-room and found an old lady lying on the sofa. I thought it was Grandma at first, but she was more like Mom, only older. Her head was propped up with pillows and the quilt was across her legs. She said she'd been calling for ages and would I please get her a glass of water?

I switched the light on in the kitchen and found Dad sitting at the table. He had thin white hair and lots of wrinkles. There were tears pouring down his face, so I asked what the matter was. He held out his hand and said it hurt, worse than any pain he'd ever had, and he couldn't even wiggle his fingers.

He said something about arthritis and that maybe some aspirin would help, but when he stood up and waved that hand at me, I could see it was the Iron Claw. I backed out into the living-room and Mom said *Where's my water?* Dad was moaning in this thin weird voice, all about how he couldn't get the top off the aspirin bottle and wasn't it his night for a sponge bath?

I tried to tell Mom I was sorry about the water, but she wasn't lying on the sofa anymore. Dad's hand looked even worse, all stiff and strange with yellow-green bruises and big purple veins. I glanced down and saw somebody had zipped me into a spongy brown dress with matching trousers. My feet looked bumpy and felt sore. I was wearing the same kind of fuzzy slippers Grandma used to wear.

I ran past the mirror and hid in my room. Dad started scratching at the door, calling out Mom's name and asking for tea and aspirin and sponge baths. I covered my ears with my hands, and after a while he stopped.

When I opened the door again, he was gone. There were just a lot of pictures in the living-room. Of Dad, Mom, Grandma, Peggy, Rudy, and loads and loads of dark-haired kids and grown-ups who reminded me of the Petraglias. I was there too, but after a while some skinny old lady I didn't recognise took my place next to Mom and Dad.

I went into the kitchen and emptied the fridge and the pantry. Then I started to cook. It's nearly ready now. Sausage rolls. Fried egg sandwiches. Macaroni and cheese. I'm going to pour myself a glass of milk, sit down at the table and eat it all, with a big scoop of ice cream and half a jar of peanut butter for dessert. Maybe then I won't feel so hungry.

But I won't go back to sleep. I'll just sit here waiting to see what happens next.

Monsieur Mallarmé Changes Names

Michèle Roberts

Until lack of inspiration threatened him with despair and disaster at the very peak of his career, Monsieur Mallarmé was a happy man. He was a poet. For many years he wrote prolifically and with increasing renown. He spent his days shifting words around, up and down, to and fro, from one line to another; he was obsessed with moving their places about on the page, he was constantly tossing them up and down in the palm of his hand like jacks or dice. He re-arranged them like red and blue and purple anemones de Caen in a vase or *mâche* and *pissenlit* salad leaves on a plate. He wrote them down on pieces of paper which he then tore up and threw out of the window so that he could watch the fragments whirl off over the boulevards; proper *flâneurs*. He dreamed of a page in perpetual motion, a scribing machine which would compose poems whose order of words changed frequently according to a secret pre-arranged rhythm so that the poem would be different on each reading and no one could claim to recognize the realest or truest version. Poems were like white swans beating their wings and they were like white marble tombstones tenderly memorializing dead friends. The images for poems, let alone the poems themselves, danced about on his tongue and spilled down onto any writing surface that presented itself: his shirt cuff, his table napkin, the inside of his wife's wrist which he would suddenly seize and inscribe with the invisible ink of his fingertip during a walk in the forest of Fontainebleau.

Their summer house was at Valvins, just outside Paris. It perched on the very edge of the Seine, which flowed past the bottom of their garden. The forest bristled on the far shore. When Mallarmé wasn't strolling along its green alleys, he was tacking up and down the broad river in his small sailing-boat. His wife and daughter, wearing loose linen clothes and straw hats, sat in the garden in basket-chairs, reading and sewing, or they weeded the flowerbeds surrounding the gravelled walks of espaliered apples that criss-crossed the grass. Friends arrived from the city to visit on Sundays, and were given lunch outside at a table set in the shade, covered with a white cloth, and adorned with jugs of roses. They ate *crudités* of radishes and shaved carrots and celery from the *potager*, roast chicken, and *patisserie*. Vuillard came, and Manet and Degas. Once out here in the countryside, they felt off-duty, and could relax. There was a kind of mental unbuttoning of shirt collars and loosening of ties that went on. They could play bowls and croquet, eat as many redcurrant tarts as they wanted, go for a sail in the little boat, smoke endless cigarettes, flirt gently with the Mallarmé ladies, and sprawl at ease in the sunshine sipping coffee and liqueurs.

When they visited the Mallarmés in Paris, at their third-floor flat in the rue de Rome, it was a much more formal affair. Mallarmé was conscious of being the most famous and respected poet of his day, of having a reputation for genius to live up to. He was a kind of unofficial laureate – the prince of poets, elected by his peers – and took his responsibilities fervently. He received his guests at his regular Tuesday evening salon, after dinner, a ritual event which became famous for the high seriousness of the discourse on offer, the fragrant crowdedness of the little dining room packed with men smoking pipes and cigars, and the excellence of the hot lemon-flavoured rum punch spiked with cloves. Mallarmé would lean against the marble mantelpiece and deliver disquisitions on literature and art and everybody felt obliged to be really intelligent and well-informed on the cultural issues of the day in case they were asked to comment. Whereas weekending in Valvins they could be childish if they wanted, they could lie on their backs on the grass, they could doze off and say nothing at all, or they could crack *risqué* jokes and tell bawdy stories, they could feel peacefully and comfortably themselves. At Valvins they were not required to ponder the nature of linguistic symbols or the relationship between music and painting, or to discuss the role of the omniscient narrator in the modern novel. The decisions that had to be made were of a less elevated order: whether to allow oneself another glass of *vin blanc cassis*, whether to suggest a piano duet to Madame Mallarmé, whether to go fishing. The painters often worked while they were down, and this for them was of course a form of pleasure. Vuillard, for example, produced three small oils of the house seen from the garden, while Degas made sketches of his hostess peeling vegetables and doing the ironing. Everyone understood that if Mallarmé needed to get on with some writing, he would slip away to his study upstairs and no one would mind. During his absences they were very well entertained by the two ladies of the household, the pretty mother and her beautiful daughter.

The house was small, shoebox-shaped, buried in its leafy, hedged garden brimming with flowering creepers and arches of roses. Downstairs was the damp kitchen, and the cellars smelling of wine and earth, upstairs the dining room and a couple of bedrooms, one for the two women, and the other for Mallarmé. His bed stood in one corner, and his desk under the window looking out over the Seine. A small glass-fronted bookcase held his collection of works in English. He was fond of the works of Edgar Allan Poe and the detective stories of Sir Arthur Conan Doyle. One door connected to the dining room, and another to the tiny landing and thence to his wife and daughter's room, with its shared bed and chest and washstand. He had a rocking-chair, brought back from his trip to London years before, set in front of the small fireplace, and here he would sit, pipe in mouth and papers on knee, writing, crossing-out, re-writing, cancelling, until summoned for dinner or lunch.

The Mallarmé family spent two or three months at Valvins every year. Mallarmé would run up to town now and then to visit his great friend, Mme Méry Laurent, the celebrated actress who was now retired from the stage but not from any of her enjoyments. In her day she had been a famous beauty, and in Stéphane Mallarmé's eyes, she still was. She was as tall and amplebodied as he, with curly hair of undiminished gold and almond-shaped grey eyes. They would eat luncheon together in her opulent apartment, sitting side by side on carved chairs at a massive table under a lampshade ballooning as pink and frilly as Méry's underskirts, sipping icy champagne while a maid served them with *pâté de foie gras* or oysters or lobster or *petits pois à la crème*, depending on the exact moment in the season and the whim of Méry's cook. After spending the afternoon in bed together they would drive in the Bois or stroll in the park, ending up at a favourite café to meet friends for gossip and drinks.

The latest craze among the painters was the new science of photography. Degas, for example, made portraits of all his intimates, including one of Stéphane and Méry dressed up in Auvergnat peasant costumes, holding walking-sticks, posed against a backdrop of crags and waterfalls. Mallarmé was fascinated by the technique required for developing the image on the photographic plate, which he compared to the swimming up of a poem into consciousness.

He had not been able to realize the invention he dreamed of, the page which would keep moving, endlessly re-forming the poem into different shapes. He was suddenly sick of writing mysterious and perfect sonnets. But he was stuck, as fixed as any page in any book folded and gathered and stitched. He could not see how to move forward, how to discover and reach his next goal. To outsiders his life appeared enviably easy and trouble-free, even luxurious: he had a flat in Paris and a country retreat in Valvins, a small private income and hence no real money worries, a devoted wife and daughter, an affectionate and accomplished mistress, several good close friends, a host of admirers and disciples, a sailing-boat, he could afford good wine and food and tobacco, he was in robust health.

The only problem was that he could no longer write poetry, did not know what to write or how to write, did not even want to write.

He said to Méry: I'm a failure. I'm finished.

He was lying in her bed in her second-floor flat in the rue St Honoré, lolling apparently very much at his ease, propped on a heap of lace-edged pillows, the apricot silk sheets rumpled around his naked chest, one arm flung up behind his head, one hand holding a cigar. An open bottle of champagne stood on the night-table; which was draped with a fringed gypsy shawl in pink and green silk. Above the bed a magnificent baldaquin unloosed falls of golden brocade which poured down around the hills of pillows and cushions and were looped back with strings of large fake pearls. The bed was very much Méry's stage. It was where she displayed her talent for seduction, occasionally hammed up, to amuse him, with flashing eyes and tossed-back hair, it was where she made her nightly appearance, magnificently nude apart from her make-up and her amber earrings, it was where she acted out her devotion to her *cher* Stéphane and recited charming speeches of passion, it was where she played the *coquette*, the *soubrette*, the *midinette*, but never the tragic heroine, where when she felt it necessary to rescue a weak performance she produced clever simulations of ecstasy, where she danced for Mallarmé, sang to him, dandled him, told him stories, did strip-tease, made him laugh, and generally convinced him that while he was in it, this was the very centre of the universe.

He lay in her bed watching her get dressed. The golden sunlight of late afternoon slipped under the lowered blinds and lay on the yellow carpet. It caressed Méry's blonde hair and glowed on her shoulders and back as she bent to pull up her stockings.

– Being a failure's just another pose, she answered him: you'll have to work at it.

She twitched her garters into place and tied them. They were sewn with forget-me-nots. He had bought them for her himself as a present the day before. Watching her fingers briefly pat the blue cotton flowers, he remembered how he had taken the garters out of their tissue paper-lined box and played with them, tested them on his fingers, admiring, amused at the delight you could take in such fripperies, the seriousness with which you discriminated between these ones of rolled violet silk and these others decorated with tiny knots of black lace. She had taught him how to buy such gifts for her and he had discovered he enjoyed going with her to choose the required frivolous accessories in a warm, perfumed shop, attended by smart, well made-up young women, watching her try on gloves, flourish and twist her wrist and hesitate between lemon kid and sky-blue, he was a happy spectator as she dithered over ankle boots buttoned to the side or the front, over evening slippers with *diamanté* on the heels or without. It didn't really matter if you didn't get it right, or if you changed your mind, because the following day you could go out and purchase another pair in quite another cut or colour. It wasn't solely a question of money. Méry, had she had no money to spend on adorning herself, would still have deliberated with equal seriousness over whether to arrange dandelions in the same glass as buttercups or daisies, whether to drink her morning cup of coffee in bed or by the window, whether to whistle in the bath or to sing. Her days were rich with small decisions and she arranged and re-arranged her world with skill, pleasure and satisfaction. She was an artist of life, she composed it and re-composed it, played with it and let it change into something else every day.

'The trouble with you,' Méry said: 'is that—'

Her voice tailed dreamily off as she surveyed her reflection in the mirror. Mallarmé, watching her pull on her drawers and pick up her stays, realized that his problem could be solved. To celebrate he took her out to the Café Procope for dinner. That night he concentrated on giving her pleasure, realizing how often it was the other way around.

He returned to Valvins by the first morning train, carrying a bulging overnight bag and greeting his wife and daughter with fond kisses. After lunch, he volunteered, for the first time ever in his life, to do the washing up. Mme and Mlle Mallarmé assumed he had heatstroke and gazed at him with concern. When he insisted, they went off, whispering to each other, into the radiant, heat-filled garden, while he juggled knives and forks into jugs of soapy water, piled plates into pagoda towers, watched soap bubbles glisten on the lips of wine glasses. Afterwards, while the two women dozed in their wicker armchairs in the bee-filled sunshine, he crept upstairs into their bedroom and opened the wardrobe door.

Back in his own room, he laid out on his bed the clothes he had borrowed from Méry, and those he had filched from his wife and child. He composed a *toilette*. He arrayed himself in stays, chemise, petticoat, and cherry silk dress, he pulled on the red wig Méry sometimes used for bedroom theatricals, he made up his face and forced his feet into high heels. He walked with small neat steps up and down his study, learning to manage his skirts and move his hips appropriately, learning a new gait, a new rhythm. Finally he checked his appearance one last time in the mirror over the fireplace, approaching his reflection and then retreating from it, flirting, curtsying and gracefully extending his hand gloved in lemon kid. Stephanie Mallarmé, poetess, had been born. He sat down at the table in front of the window and began to write.

'A Throw of the Dice', Mallarmé's extraordinary experimental concrete poem, in which the text is flung and scattered and repeated in different type-sizes over successive pages, is universally recognized as his masterpiece, the patterns of dancing words evoking both chaos and a new order, the dawning of modernism, the creation of difficult beauty in the void left by God's exile. What is not so generally well known is the circumstance under which Mallarmé wrote it, dressed in women's clothes to facilitate the birth of a new kind of imagination, a radically different poetry. To put it simply: Stephanie could write things that Stéphane could not.

Degas is supposed to have made several photographic

portraits of Stephanie Mallarmé, but the plates have been lost. Some art historians think that Stephanie served as Degas' model for some of his studies of washerwomen and laundresses, but the matter remains in dispute.

Skin Sins

Sarah Johnson

A corner shop.
Paint peeled blue. Eggshell blinds thick-furred so that inside the dust must dance. Dancing as a silt-slatted screen for the person within. Should she look out.

Dust grown against a childhood where the absence of dirt gleamed bright as the knob of the clovered tap. At the point where the metal curved, Marcia, in the bath, could see herself. Face and pot belly distended, with school plaits fraying as her mother scrubbed. Gloved.

'Heavens, heavens, heavens, child. What do you do at that place?'

Marcia's mother's hand, scrubbing brush grasped, abraded Marcia's thigh until latex pink.

'Filth, filth.'

She slapped the thigh around, so it loomed raw, to start the other side.

'You know that if I could prevail upon the authorities to see it my way I would never send you?'

Marcia nodded, she had seen the letters to the school authorities on the subject of dirt. Marcia's mother scraped her hands free of the gloves and spread her fingers wide, making the bone glow in the skin.

'Rubber gloves breed germs,' Marcia recited, back to the taps trying not to clench.

'Filth,' her mother spread Marcia's buttocks and scraped her nail down the shadowed cleft which leaked off the tailbone between them.

'Filth.'

Turn again. In the tap, hair standing out as if electrified. Marcia could see the lacquered nails digging in the folds of her ears.

'The other children must have slovenly mothers.'

Marcia nodded.

'Who are they?'

Reflected, Marcia's eyes and her mother's, the question between them.

'The same, Mummy. Alison, Caroline, Lucy.'

'You know that if that teacher ever shifts you?'

'I know, Mummy.'

'You know the children I mean?'

'I know, Mummy.'

'You must promise.'

'I promise I'll tell you immediately, Mummy.'

'Good,' her mother's voice snapped upright. In the tap Marcia could see the dripping rubber gloves, shed like lacerated skins on the side of the bath.

Marcia wore white socks to school. White socks with frilled tops. She sat at the table closest to the teacher with five other prettily socked girls. The central table housed children whose grey and green socks slouched unevenly as they ran at playtime. At the back of the room was a third table. Marcia caught glimpses of its children. Stripes of caramel, graphite, beige. Ribbon patches of tinted skin, warm as fire flicker behind a grate. The teacher stood offset from the back table. Eyes slitted high and away, as if the heat seared her. The children very small beneath her drawn-up posture, her high words floating over them. Usually the teacher sat at her desk talking square on at her white-socked girls.

In spring there was a fire drill. The class was lined up at random in the playground. Marcia stood behind a back table boy. Marcia had liked the name of this boy's home when he said it in class. Nuie. Coveted the lilt of it. Liked the way it curled to a cusp at the end. Up close she saw that the boy's skin didn't flicker. It lipped matt smooth off the fold at his throat to emerge on his wrist and wrap unbroken around his fingers. It had none of the episodic flaring to pink of her own elbows and cheeks. He smelt of soap. Marcia tiptoed, peering for nail marks in his ears but the boy turned and pushed her hard in the chest, toppling her back.

'You look like chocolate,' Marcia said.

Now the boy peered at her, his eyes running quick as spiders over her face as if he had never seen her before. Marcia burnt red but the boy turned away. She was left eclipsed, all her pink and white refracted around the playground. She wanted him to turn back and see her in her white socks. She leant in close again. Hot ear close.

'I know why you're brown,' she said.

The boy did not turn.

'I know,' she repeated, 'it's because you're dirty. I know because my mother told me.'

The boy turned, suddenly he seemed much bigger than she was and his eyes were like the teacher's, going beyond her.

'Dirty, dirty,' Marcia chanted, low and insistent, wanting to burn red but with each word seeing herself fading. The boy's high eyes were squashing her so that they could never see down to where she was. Marcia knew that her mother was down here too. Down in the low insistence, some brown person had sucked up her mother and sprayed her out like pink quartz, ground to dust.

Marcia's mother cut the brown-skinned children out of Marcia's class photo where they filled the back row as an after-thought.

'Look how pale you look,' her mother's nail traced Marcia's captured limbs. 'Look how clean.'

The photos hung in the hall. Purity's role of honour. Marcia the radiating centre star, until the year she slipped and fell. In the photo the bruise newly seeping spread beneath her pulled-down skirt. Her mother's nail hovered. With a fine brush she painted out the bruise, but the white paint mottled Marcia's disarrayed flesh. Blotched thigh, alarm-red cheeks, yellow knuckles clenched on her hem. Other composed children slipped to the fore. Her mother cut her from the photo altogether. The photo hung alongside the others in the hall. Marcia a blank cardboard space in a row of smiles.

Marcia's mother ignored her. Burnt all the rubber gloves and took instead to peeling herself with the vegetable knife. Fine pink lines spiralled her arms like spun sugar candy, latticed her thighs and webbed her belly. Tracery of blood, capillaries that had fed the skin claiming the surface, red leaking into pink into blue.

'Cut out the dirt,' she admonished Marcia exposing her fingerbone to illustrate the point, 'hunt it down and cut it out.'

Marcia scrubbed herself. Punishing to rawness.

Men and an ambulance took Marcia's mother away, her arms flailing slashers.

'Filth, disgusting filth.' Red seeping through hair and cloth, spraying neighbours and escorts.

'Nowhere cleaner than a hospital, lady,' the burly

man strapped Marcia's mother down. 'Clean as a pin there.'

He closed the ambulance doors on Marcia's mother, looking out and straight through Marcia who stood digging the toe of her white sandal into the grass verge.

Alone inside the house Marcia lost sight of herself. Her body receded from her. She ran her hands over her thighs and they disappeared up to her wrists. When she moved, mosaic slits appeared, torso cleft from limb, appendicles floated off. She went out a lot.

Marcia liked the town streets full of people, happy people, swinging confidently in and out of shops like their own back doors. Energetic people. They knew what they wanted, took what they wanted. Talked in high colour. Considered in long coats over coffee, swung off, turned over, discarded.

Marcia, walking among them, could see herself reflected, brightly swimming in the shop windows. She preferred the night when the dark came down and focused on the windows. Shop lights, streetlights, car lights, winking a coloured crown, the shoppers gone, she could stand square in front of one and see herself squarely back.

In a shop doorway a woman fed her baby. Marcia stood in front of the window. Rain made the stage lights flicker. On display was a silver lamé dress, long and sleek. Marcia counted her limbs over it, spread her fingers wide, ghost-stroked the dress. The woman watched Marcia and snorted.

'I'm going to buy it,' Marcia said.

'Spoilt honky bitch,' the woman replied. The night lights flickered.

'I beg your pardon?'

'Which part didn't you understand? Honky as in white honky, honking white, white trash.'

Marcia scrutinised the woman. She could be white herself. The shop sign flashed above her. Green face, olive hair, yellow breast. The baby's scarlet lips sucked scarlet nipple. The sign flashed blue.

'Pardon.'

'So it was "spoilt" you didn't grasp. Same thing, honey. Makes you spoilt white skin. Fruit that's had too much sun turns to mush.'

The silver dress flashed aquamarine, the baby flashed peacock, the woman bundled the baby in a sapphire blanket. The shop was open so Marcia went in.

Inside, fluorescent lights shone spotlight bright. Women with her mother's nails flicked racks. The clothes swung away as Marcia approached. Marcia walked back out. The spotlight came with her. In the street were people she had never seen. Young men indigo hunched in old men's coats, people whose skin was wax creased yellow. Ginger people who stooped tired under abundant flesh, bloodless people who swung past the shops like they were other people's back doors. The woman and baby had gone.

At home Marcia sat naked in front of the television. The lights were off, the television technicolor tinted her legs.

'Hello,' she said to the game show host.

'Hello,' replied the host 'And welcome to tonight's episode of "Spin A Million".'

The host and contestants lined tooth bright across Marcia's legs.

'Hello,' she said to the news presenter.

'Good evening and welcome to the "News at Ten".'

Marcia ran her hands up her legs and over her hips. Her flesh remained solid. Her body contained folds and corners she had not known about, she fingered bony mounds, counted flaps, tested trampoline flesh.

'They must pay,' a woman on the television said.

'Who?' Marcia asked. Her hands glowed guiltily. She crossed her arms.

'The white people cannot be absolved of the responsibility for what has been done to the indigenous peoples.'

'But I haven't been out,' said Marcia.

'They must pay for the crimes of their forefathers,' the woman's face filled the screen, dark with anger.

'It was my mother who told me,' Marcia said but the woman was gone, leaving accusatory smudges on Marcia's shins.

Marcia took to touring the suburbs on the train. The train she thought was a bubble of transition, she watched how faces changed as people entered and left. She noticed the same man each day. He stood holding onto the door pole. He was graceful and swayed as the train moved. Sometimes he read a book held in his spare hand. Sometimes he just looked out the window, swaying. Marcia sat straight in her seat and watched. The pole was silver. The light through the window was smudged grey. The man was the darkest she had ever seen. His cheek was the blue of ancient buried bottles. An aubergine line rimmed his upper lip. The channel from lip to nose disappeared in the false train light, dark folded upon itself to create an opening, a space of possibility in his face.

The man noticed that Marcia watched him and eventually he kissed her.

'What colour do you call this?' she asked skimming a finger over his lip.

'Black,' he said.

'It's not,' she replied, 'it's another colour, something else less definite.'

The man's name was Joseph. He lay on the bed in the sunlight. Marcia stood naked in the bathroom door.

'Come out', Joseph said. His limbs were long and smooth and full. His creased and curving places were shaded to obscurity, then blossomed out, changing shape as he moved. Something always hidden. The sunlight ran off him in flat plains. He was a blue-black violet river on the bed. He was a definite place. Marcia's own body seemed unformed in comparison. A series of questions. An eye corner phantom. She dared not come out.

Joseph came to fetch her.

'Beautiful,' he said drawing her limbs with strong strokes. Marcia lay still. Felt exposed.

'Beautiful'.

Marcia's scars rose to the surface under the strokes. There were the channels of her mother's nails, the chest pushing hand, the TV woman, the scrubbed and spat places. Her body proclaimed her secrets like an anatomical drawing. She felt ashamed. Joseph ran a questioning finger between her buttocks.

'What is this?' he asked.

'Black,' Marcia said.

'Yes,' Joseph replied, 'black is not only to do with colour.'

They lay on the bed side by side. The sun had gone. They lay in the negative of the moon. Boundaries merged and ran.

'Come travel with me?' Joseph asked, 'We will go to the two extremes.'

Marcia thought it best.

They went first to the northern lands. The sunlight came

from very far up over steps of fibrous cloud. The people were the colour of beach-bleached bone, with angled cheeks and shoulders that ended in the square folds of clothes. Marcia and Joseph looked at the buildings. Beautiful old buildings, soft and painted by weather, they glowed the gentle golden sun of accumulated years. The people walked between the buildings in the rarefied sun. It was as if the buildings strung them up, with the age of them, kept them true and square, seeing only the buildings and the age and the history. Buoyed on their mutual past.

Marcia and Joseph stood on the banks of the Thames, their toes overhanging the concrete lip. One side of the city branched across and touched the other, the river moving slow and thick between.

'This is where I grew up,' Joseph said. 'When I was young I loved the bridges. On Sundays I would walk along here with my mother and draw them, one each week. After I had finished all the bridges I drew the buildings, then the gates and the steps and the wharves. This river was magic to me.'

Marcia thought of the small blue-black boy and his mother in the angular Sunday crowds. Out strolling in the old gold light. Sliding around the pair like dark river stones.

'In this country you can choose to be anonymous,' Joseph said, guessing her thoughts. 'Not then but later I chose it. The people see you, a black man and they don't know what to think. They possess many differing myths and are confused. I gave them no clues and they left me alone.'

Marcia went to buy a paper. The kiosk was at the base of Big Ben. The newspaper seller's face was as grey-folded as the tabloids he sold.

'You've got the best spot,' Marcia said, handing him coins.

'Aye,' the man grunted, his eyes flicking dismissively off the golden tower. 'Bloody racket when it chimes though.'

He scrutinised Marcia. 'You a tourist then?' he asked.

'Yes, I guess so.'

'Don't mind you lot, not at all; it's the other kinds I can't stomach.'

'What do you mean?' Marcia asked.

The newspaper seller glanced to where Joseph stood.

'Problem with this country,' he said, 'is there's too many bloody foreigners. Should go back where they came from.'

Marcia and Joseph stood on the edge of the Thames watching its sluggish flow. Many people walked past and did not heed them. The aged sun sank until the buildings swallowed it. Its last rays shone in spears from behind the facades. They shot through the people and plunged in the sluggish brown water, throwing back a smutty river haze. Joseph pointed to it.

'What colour do you call that?' he asked.

'It's nothing that I recognise,' Marcia replied.

They went to the African lands. They stood barefoot on the edge of the savannah, their toes pointing east. The sun cracked the horizon spilt red at dawn. It shone beyond colour at noon drawing up the ochre earth through desiccated trees whose mandarin leaves leaked the sky. Marcia felt fractured and brittle beneath it. Many people walked vast distances, space surrounding them.

'This is the first time in my life that I have not felt the odd one out,' said Joseph, but Marcia felt he slipped from her. The sun warped the horizon and Joseph's boundaries blurred without the contrast of difference. Many people passed and he walked unnoticed. She felt she came hard up against them. She looked in the people's eyes and felt the responsibility of generations of misplaced white women. The people looked at her and saw tight lines on the supple sky.

'I must leave,' she said to Joseph. 'This is your place and I am keeping you from it.'

'Marcia,' Joseph replied, 'I am from London. This is where my parents are from, this is not my place.'

She left anyhow.

Marcia followed the continent down and around. Her skin shed from her as she went. Underneath rose her scars, hard fibrous ridges of scrape, push and accuse. As they rose, she reclaimed them. Using a needle sterilised in flame and ink the colour of bruise she picked them out. Pricking the fine skin and easing the ink in, they spanned her limbs like ropes of a vine.

Her route ringed the Indian Ocean. She passed through lands where the people glowed ruddy as sun setting in cold air. Lands where people assumed the shades they walked through. People whose skins were translucent, swirled, burnt and scored. Numberless people with their own lives, thoughts and preoccupations. None of which involved her. None of whom noticed her pass. It reassured her.

In Asia she held out her hands to a woman in azure silk whose own hands were cool as stone. The woman used a feather to lace Marcia's knuckles and palms with henna tattoos. Jubilant orange. Over days they faded.

Marcia went back. 'Please make them permanent,' she asked, holding out her hands to the tattooist. The woman took them firmly, slid a finger up Marcia's inner arm, circled the joint's blue pulse of blood. The azure silk winked.

'Not yet,' she said. 'We do not mark our own bodies lightly. Stay awhile, you must be ready to choose your pattern.'

Marcia sat in the shadows of the tattooist's tent. She watched the people come and choose their marks. She watched the tattooist at her work, how she closed her eyes when the customers described what they wanted, how she stroked the skin's nap, the needles she chose, the tautness stretched for the initial prick, the depth that she pierced. Marcia ground the powders for the inks. Salts and stones. Fine dried flowers, their colours preserved in oris root, so intense they hurt. Crystallised waters, tubers and oils, adding pinches of saffron and gold at the last moment. As she worked, her clothes lifted, revealing her own purple lines. The tattooist rested a hand there.

'I see you already have some marks,' she said. 'I doubt you chose them.'

As the seasons changed so too did the tattoos. As the trees lost their leaves spaces appeared in the designs, with the rains came softness and hues of blue varied beyond imagining.

'We are recording parts of people's stories,' the azure woman stated. 'Things do not happen in vacuums and nor do people's decisions as to which story they will choose to represent them. The time of the choice must be incorporated in the tattoo.'

'It is a hard decision,' Marcia replied. 'Which story to tell the world about.'

'Yes,' said the azure woman. 'But stories grow with the telling and it is better than letting others choose your story for you.'

Some customers said nothing when they came. The

tattooist laid them on the cotton plinth. She ran her cool hands over their bodies.

'You must learn to read the skin's patterns,' she said to Marcia. 'It is easy once you understand them; you just trace what they say.'

Marcia watched the tattooist's hands, watched where they rested, where they probed, but she saw only the bodies. The beautiful bodies gleaming nakedly on the plinth. Contour and hillock, recessed and secretive. She fed on them. Rejoiced in them. Read what their tattoos, once laid, had chosen to say.

A young woman came to the tent. She stood in the shadows hesitantly. Her eyes were themselves shadows. She chewed her lips, rimmed in red sores. The tattooist did not turn the woman away, as she had other hesitant people, but led her to the plinth. Marcia gently bathed the woman's rigid body. As she washed, she saw the impression of a hand on the woman's face, in the small of her back a boot imprint – three years' past, planted hard. In the woman's feet was a childhood summer in the sun, in her belly a string of abortions, the babies all named. Marcia read of fatigue and distrust, night-time fears, coveted food and below it all the hot feet running wild in ash-hot sand. She cleaned the woman's sores.

The tattooist took a long time over the young woman. When she had finished Marcia saw only a buried trace of tattoo. Around the woman's navel a ring of shells clustered, nebulous beneath a carpet of golden belly sand. In each shell a tiny form could be made out, a twist, a *koru*, an unborn curl of child held safe and compact. The sand shifted and the form was concealed. The woman was asleep. The tattooist looked at Marcia over her belly.

'I think you are ready for your own tattoos,' she said.

Marcia mixed her inks. She chose azure jewelled. An

undertone of orange, an overtone of sage. Highlights of lemon, glints of magenta. A slippery shiny ink, an ink of question and desire. She lay on the plinth. The tattooist read her slowly. She kneaded the sinews and scars, left no part untraced. Then she began. Pale deserts covered Marcia's feet and toes, from her insteps thick trees sprung foresting her shins. Winking neon stars scattered her chest. Flowers and leaves embellished her old purple vines.

'Someone has found a place here,' the tattooist said, etching a strong outline where Joseph's hand had first fallen. 'He will come to reclaim it.'

Using ochre earth she reapplied the henna hand tattoos. She mixed a hot red fire ink.

'A gift,' she said and in the shadow of Marcia's tailbone she drew a snake, its sharp tipped tail disappearing between Marcia's buttocks.

'I have just begun the story,' she said as Marcia left. 'You must continue it yourself.'

Marcia travelled on. Her body was her palette to record the things she saw. A man stopped to hoe her hip, a child ran her palm. Flowers of many lands sprouted on her vines, tropical and alpine oddly neighboured. Beasts she had heard of, beasts she had seen, emotions she awaited patterned her limbs. On her inner thighs she tattooed a private sea. Crested waves broke on her knees, becalmed estuaries lapped her groin. With a needle as fine as child's hair she tattooed her vulva scarlet. Colour of shame, the blue deepened it, gave other, softer meanings. Marcia accepted, frilling her labia with a patina of yellow. Coral and shell afloat.

At night her fingers Braille-read the tales she had written. Some she amended, some unfinished, others joined to form connections. She travelled on, headed south. She headed home. When she arrived, the patterns of land and sky would fall differently on her and she had something to say in return. Messages of her own to leave in other people's skin.

On the corner is Marcia's tattoo shop. Paint peeled blue.

Inside the dust dances, a silt-slatted screen should she look out. As customers approach, the delicate tracery on Marcia's hands begins to tingle. Energy of anticipation. The needle and the prick. She waits for them in the shadow. Her customers cannot make her out in the dim interior but feel calmed by her beautiful henna hands. She lays them on the table. She reads what they have brought to tell her. They see that she wears clothes of the finest white muslin, through which her body appears to shift and change. They cannot quite grasp it, but as she works Marcia leans out of the shadow. A ray comes through the blinds and then they see, when the dusty spotlight hits her, that she has skin the colour of jewels, vivid, winking, a mosaic beneath her clothes. Marcia shifts and it is gone.

Girls in their Loveliness

Ann Jolly

John McEwan met Violet Cameron at Cameron's Hotel when he came to Kinchurdy on oil business. There wasn't anywhere else for him to stay unless you counted B & B at Mary Murray's and very little fun there was to be had there with Mary being Wee Free and having nothing to do with the drink at all. She was none too good a cook either and it was rumoured she served her guests packet soup and tinned mince. So John McEwan stayed at Cameron's Hotel and very soon afterwards he stayed in Violet Cameron's bed. He was a fine looking man with a full head of dark hair and a briefcase stuffed with important papers. For so masculine a person he had surprising hands – clean and smallish – not like the big cracked hands of the farmers who came into Cameron's Hotel for a wee refreshment on a Saturday evening before the Kirk or the Wee Free Church or Chapel with Father O'Brien on Sunday mornings, hypocrites all. Violet Cameron could confirm that. Didn't she serve them whisky and fend off their groping hands and watch them in their dark suits with their clean fat wives on their arms and their children behind them as they paraded on Sundays as if their souls were as white as their dentures?

In the fifties in the harsh north-east of Scotland a woman was judged by the quality of her daughters and found wanting if they were not wholesome and pure.

Women were to be chaste, comely and good mothers and their daughters to be chaste, comely and good. But when you have shown a girl her loveliness there is no turning back. Once she knows the power of her face and body a girl is changed for ever. That's where John McEwan's wife, Kate, was so clever.

Violet Cameron considered herself sophisticated, a cut above the other women in Kinchurdy and they despised her for running a hotel with a bar and wearing suede high-heeled shoes with petersham bows and American tan stockings. Despite this handicap Violet was determined that her daughters should be respectable, a credit to her upbringing, a reflection of their mother's superior status and one in the eye for her critics. Her husband, Willie Cameron, had died aged forty-two, a great relief to Violet for it had been difficult to hold her head up in Bairds the Butchers or Stewarts' Fresh Fruit and Veg knowing people were aware that her man drank to excess. Having a fatal heart attack in the early hours of a Sunday morning brought on by love of the malt and lust for a young woman working at table during the summer season had been one of the few productive things Willie Cameron had done in Violet's view – apart from fathering her daughters, that is.

'He was a good man. Violet Cameron will have her work cut out running the hotel without him,' men said to one another at the funeral.

No decent woman went to a burial. That was man's work, as was the lamenting afterwards at the bar of Cameron's Hotel where they were served by the grieving widow. Women mourned in private. Alcohol was a potent weapon in the Devil's armoury but they weren't averse to a little tipple now and then if the occasion demanded it when their cheeks, usually the colour of sour cream, would turn to frugal rose. Violet didn't bother with their pretence, she sipped vodka and lime behind the bar, sherry in the kitchen and whisky in her bedroom after the hotel closed for the night. But her daughters were to be different. Morag and I were sheltered, kept away from the evils of drink and whatever it was that went on in the public bar. Violet screeched at us if we so much as dabbed at ourselves with her perfume or rolled over the waistbands on our school skirts, thus inflaming local boys with the sight of our scabbed knees.

Violet Cameron couldn't get enough of John McEwan. Respectable women didn't enjoy sex. Violet wasn't respectable. Other women wore corsets to hold in their flesh, using the pink boned fabric to conceal and repel. Violet wore underwear to enhance and entice, circle-stitched brassières like ice cream cones sticking to her chest and elastic panty girdles giving a smooth line to her buttocks under her too tight, too short skirts. John McEwan's visits had her painting her toenails scarlet and spraying scent across the bed sheets so that they wouldn't smell of whisky and stale cigarettes and goodness knows what else. John and Violet would drink together in the bar and when Violet had called Last Orders a good deal more promptly than usual, they would fall up the back stairs to her bedroom clutching a bottle of Bell's Whisky. Morag and I would hear them laughing and grunting into the night. At fourteen I had only a vague idea of what was happening but Morag, two years older, would hide her head under her pillow and cry, whether for shame or hurt I couldn't tell.

In the beginning John McEwan came to Kinchurdy once a quarter on oil business, then every two months, then monthly. I think he was as hot for my mother as she was for him. It must have been obvious to the customers of Cameron's Hotel what was happening and the information would have been passed on and relished in Kinchurdy town. That sort of news travelled faster than a gorse fire on the hill and John McEwan's wife, Kate, got wind of it down there in Glasgow, for one day she stepped off the train with her husband. Violet had known of her coming, for her lover had booked a double room and she had been shouting and screaming at us all week before the couple arrived. John McEwan looked uncomfortable and clearly had had little say in his wife's decision to visit Kinchurdy. Equally clearly he was not prepared to abandon his carefully constructed and sexually deficient life with Kate in Glasgow for passion with the unpredictable Violet Cameron in Kinchurdy. So she had to simmer and sulk while Kate sat in the dining room, gazing admiringly at her husband, waving her frosted finger tips in the air and laughing at his jokes.

Morag and I were very taken with Kate McEwan.

'She's just like a film star,' Morag said, though not in Violet's hearing.

Kate McEwan was all subtlety and restraint. We hardly noticed that she set out to charm us. She had curled fair hair, a soft peachy skin and wore smart little suits in beige and sand. She talked to us as though we were grown up, flicking through magazines to show us pictures of women with crimson mouths and full-skirted swirling frocks.

'This is pretty, that red would suit you, Morag, with your dark colouring,' and Morag would blush and pull at the frayed cuffs of her school blouse.

'Have you tried tying your hair back?' She collected my brown frizzy mop in her pale hand and pulled it off my face. 'It suits you'.

'I've no children of my own but if I could choose I would have two girls just like you.'

Ann Jolly

She wove a spell around us. Two naive country lasses, we were easy meat. We had been led to believe that dressing up or putting Pond's cold cream on our faces made us common as muck; that boys were dangerous and we risked being burnt to a crisp in hell if we lost our reputations by so much as talking to any of the clodhopping young men hanging around the Italian café with the juke box on a Saturday evening. With a mother like Violet Cameron and her 'Don't do as I do, do as I say' we were almost branded as outcasts already and were ripe for seduction by clever Kate McEwan with her interest and her compliments.

Violet convinced herself that Kate couldn't have been half so nice to us if she had had an inkling of what her husband and Violet got up to when John McEwan was in Kinchurdy on his own. But I think Kate McEwan had a very good idea of what was happening. I suspect she didn't mind about the sex. She never struck me as the sort of woman for whom that was important. She wanted to be admired for her femininity and style and to have the power that her sexuality and her husband's income gave her, the act itself was not as crucial a barometer of what was going on as Violet wished to believe. But Kate wasn't going to be upstaged or outmanoeuvred, nor relinquish John McEwan and his salary to Violet, a woman she made plain she thought of as a common tart. She also had the advantage over Violet in that she didn't drink: 'Not good for my skin.'

She drew one of her petal soft hands across a silky cheek, letting her fingertip rest at the corner of her mouth. Morag and I watched as she outlined her lips with a little brush, rubbing the colour onto it from Apricot Blush lipstick in a gold case with a mirror that flicked up. Then she coated her lips and blotted them on a piece of hotel toilet paper before pouting at us, 'What do you think?'

Morag and I nodded. We were entranced. This was how women should be. So Kate McEwan hooked and reeled us in.

John McEwan continued to stay regularly at Cameron's Hotel and Kate began to come with him now and then. Morag and I looked forward to her visits though we knew better than to say anything to Violet who was always in a foul mood when a double room in the name of Mr and Mrs McEwan was reserved. It meant that she and John had to snatch their pleasure where they could and Morag and I were spared those whisky-tainted nights next door to Violet's bedroom.

'I've been thinking,' said Kate after two or three visits, 'how would you both like to come and stay with me in Glasgow during the holidays?'

'Yes,' we said, 'yes, please.'

Violet took a little persuading that a week in Glasgow for her two girls with John McEwan's wife was a good thing. I think she was torn between losing our labour in the hotel, not having to guard our chastity during the school holidays and letting her precious daughters spend time with her lover's wife. Even Violet could see this arrangement had its strange side. A week without the responsibility of daughters won and John took us back to Glasgow after his next stay in Kinchurdy.

It was a wonderful week. Kate fussed and looked after us in a totally unfamiliar way. We even had breakfast in bed one morning and Kate came and sat on the edge of Morag's bed wrapped in an almond green silk kimono covered in blowsy roses. She smelled of roses too.

'Today I think we'll go shopping. If you're to go to the Tennis Club Dance at the end of the week, then you'll need something to wear.'

Morag and I looked at each other. Dance, what dance? In our world dancing was a short cut to ruination but when Kate left we practised cavorting across the cream carpet in our pyjamas, holding one another like we'd seen at the pictures until we fell on my bed giggling and breathless with the excitement of it all.

Kate put a great deal of effort into improving our appearance for the Saturday dance. We went to the hairdressers and she made us try on clothes by the armful, studying them all carefully, neat fair head on one side until she was satisfied. On Saturday morning she played waltzes and fox-trots on the radiogram and we practised dancing with each other and with John McEwan until Kate was content that we would not disgrace her if by some miracle a boy asked us to dance.

But in the evening when I looked in the mirror I knew that boys would be falling over themselves to dance with us for Kate had transformed us. My hair had been trimmed and the frizz coaxed into curls that shone and waved where Kate had tied them on top of my head with a blue ribbon to match my dress. The dress had a tight bodice and four yards of material in the skirt that rippled over paper nylon petticoats so stiff I made a crackling noise when I moved. But if I was good to look at, Morag was stunning. Her dress was straight, crimson, with a fishtail pleat that fanned out behind her as she walked in her new high heels and you couldn't help but notice her bottom and her legs. An Alice band held her black hair off her face and it fell like a dark waterfall down her back.

Kate admired her handiwork, 'I know just how to finish you off.'

I thought we were finished but I got a touch of pink lipstick and there was red for Morag. Then Kate took a block of mascara and got Morag to spit on it before she brushed her eyelashes so that they were longer and curlier than before and Morag's eyes looked bigger and browner than ever. John McEwan whistled when he saw us, Morag blushed and Kate gave a funny little tight smile. Violet Cameron would have burst a blood vessel if she had seen her daughters at that moment.

'I'll just come and introduce you to a few people,' Kate said as the taxi drew up at the tennis club. Light was shining through the pavilion windows and the sound of a band thumped in the suburban evening every time the door opened.

'John and I will be back to collect you at eleven,' Kate said and Morag and I were catapulted into another world.

The young men were a million miles from the farmers' sons in Kinchurdy. These young men had been to private schools and wore blazers with braid around the lapels. They smelled of Brylcreem and beer and when they talked to one another it was of rugby, golf and tennis, not football, the price of animal feed and whether they could get the hay in before the weather broke. We looked just like the other girls there though Morag was prettier. Kate had known what she was doing.

We were new faces and popular with the boys. I had only just learned to dance but was transparently enthusiastic and didn't lack for partners. The floor was so thick with people you didn't have to be a good dancer anyway and the crowd was an excuse for Ronnie or James or Chas to dance with his body pressed up against mine and breathe heavily in my ear. Caught up in the thrill of it I lost sight of Morag until the band took a break and a rock'n'roll record was played. A few couples got up to dance, among them Morag holding the hand of a boy whose fair hair fell across his face as they jived. I hadn't known Morag could jive. Unaware of anything going on around them, they took up more and more space until other couples pulled back from the circle they had created as they spun and whirled. Morag's hair was flying out behind her and her cheeks were the colour of her dress. The record ended and people clapped, the boy put both arms around Morag and kissed her on the lips and she closed her eyes and kissed him back.

Too late, Violet Cameron, too late, your daughters have seen their loveliness, they are awake.

When Kate and John McEwan came to collect us, Morag pulled the fair-haired boy over to introduce him, 'Rob'. We shook hands, his palm was hot and sweaty but he had a nice smile. John and Kate already knew his family and Rob gave Morag his address on a piece of paper.

'Remember to write,' he said as we left.

From the look on her face it didn't seem likely Morag would forget.

After Glasgow, Kinchurdy was dull. Violet was drinking more than ever and her temper fluctuated alarmingly. Morag and I slaved in the kitchen and dining room for the remainder of the holidays, our mother having alienated almost everyone else who might have taken work in Cameron's Hotel. Occasionally we slipped up to our room and tried on The Dresses, frightened that their magic would slip away. Morag and Rob wrote to one another, she showed me bits of his letters but mostly she kept them to herself, reading and re-reading them before locking them in an old black cash box, the only privacy Violet allowed her.

Then a letter was received from Kate and John McEwan; they were coming to spend time in Kinchurdy and would require one double and one single room. They were bringing a young friend with them whose name was Rob! Morag did her chores for the week before their arrival in a happy daze; even Violet noticed. 'Well, it's good to see someone cheerful around here.'

I suspect she was distracted by worrying about how she could get together with John McEwan if his wife was on the scene or she might have commented on the loving care with which Morag prepared the single room on the upper floor for Rob. She certainly knew nothing of the note that Morag left under the pillow.

The McEwans and Rob were at Cameron's Hotel for just three nights and Morag didn't sleep in our room for any of those nights. She almost trusted me to keep her secret but threw in a few threats as well.

'If you tell her about me and Rob I'll never do your maths homework again and . . . and I'll cut up your dress.'

She needn't have bothered. Romantic love with a boy as good-looking as Rob, even second-hand, was so alluring compared with our everyday lives that nothing would have induced me to expose her. Besides, I loved Morag, it was the one pure uncomplicated relationship that I had and I wouldn't have jeopardised it under any circumstances. I think Kate knew, in fact I'm certain she did, but she colluded with me in keeping what was going on from Violet. Rob and Morag spent every possible moment together during his stay and I covered for her whenever I could, doing most of her work as well as my own. Then Rob and the McEwans went back to Glasgow.

Morag ran away three months later. I'm almost sure she put some of Violet's sleeping pills in my bedtime drink that night because I never heard her leave. She was there when I went to sleep and when I woke up she'd gone. The bed looked as if she had just lain on it for a little and only her school uniform was left in the wardrobe. Violet was distraught, storming and ranting about 'my little girl, my beautiful daughter' and she had to go to the police station to report it which was a terrible disgrace. I was subjected to an inquisition from her and from Sergeant McBride but I never dropped a hint about what I knew or guessed. In Kinchurdy nobody's business was their own, so Sergeant McBride must have had a fair idea of the difficulties of our family life and it was several days before he cranked himself up to take serious action about Morag's disappearance. By that time a postcard with a picture of Kelvingrove Art Galleries in Glasgow had arrived. On the back Morag had written, 'I am fine and am going to stay here. Please do not come and look for me. Love Morag'

It was to be nearly ten years before I saw my sister again. We were writing to one another by the time she emigrated to Australia but I couldn't get down to London where she was living to see her off; it cost too much and I was running Cameron's Hotel and protecting Violet from herself almost single-handedly by then. Violet still queened it over the bar and issued orders to any staff I could afford but I'm not being conceited when I say the business would have fallen apart without me.

Morag came to Kinchurdy for our mother's funeral. She had been back from Melbourne for a couple of months by then but had only got as far as London when Violet fell in a drunken stupor from the platform at Kinchurdy Station in front of the night train to Inverness. I don't know why she had taken to going down there in the evenings although I wondered if, when she'd had a few drinks, she turned the clock back in her head and thought there might be a chance of meeting John McEwan on his way to Cameron's Hotel. There was a fatal accident inquiry and talk of suicide but the Procurator Fiscal returned a verdict of Death by Misadventure and I was spared the shame of having to bury Violet in unconsecrated ground.

So for the first time in ten years Morag and I sat together at the kitchen table in Cameron's Hotel. We drank tea and filled in the gaps in our knowledge of one another's lives. She confirmed what I had already guessed, that she had been pregnant when she fled Kinchurdy. With nowhere else to go she had turned up on the McEwans' doorstep and Kate had taken her in. Kate had also helped her get rid of the baby – Morag shuddered at this part of the story – then found her work as an artist's model. I already knew about the modelling for I had read Morag's letters to Violet who had given the impression around Kinchurdy that her daughter was a mannequin in a big department store. Our mother wasn't going to give local folk the satisfaction of knowing that Morag Cameron took her clothes off so that students of both sexes could draw her naked. There had been other men for Morag since Rob but none engaged her heart or matched that first flowering of adult love. It had been a man that had taken her to Australia, his desertion that brought her back.

I asked after Kate McEwan, did she still keep in touch?

'No.'

For all that Kate had been so helpful when Morag was in trouble and mixed up about her feelings for Rob and his betrayal, for he had said the baby couldn't possibly be his, Morag didn't want to know her any more. She had begun to suspect Kate of not caring what happened to her, of only using her as a weapon in the war with Violet over John McEwan. So Morag had devised her own revenge and gone to bed with John McEwan – Kate's husband and Violet's lover.

'It wasn't difficult to tempt him,' Morag said, 'he always was one for a bit on the side.'

She gave a small closed-up smile, crossed her elegant legs and smoothed her short tight skirt towards her knees.

I recalled Violet's appetite for John McEwan and looked again at Morag. For a moment it seemed I was seeing our mother – or was it Kate McEwan? – sitting there across from me at the table in the kitchen of the hotel.

'It wasn't very exciting,' she said, 'I don't know what either of them saw in him, he was nothing in bed,' dismissively she tapped ash from her cigarette into the empty cup with a red tipped nail, 'but I made damn sure that Kate knew what had happened.'

'Now, tell me about you.'

The Lighthouse Keeper's Wife

Helen Dunmore

She'd gone. She hadn't waited for him.

Nancy always waited for him. She believed that there would always be a good reason if he was late. Not like his sister May. May thought disaster had come if she had to wait ten minutes for Jack to meet her outside the Stores. She'd look at her pocket-watch, glance up the street, shake her watch busily, as if it might not be working. May believed the worst, then drew it to herself. She'd had money since she married Jack, and she lived in town as she'd always wanted, but it made no difference.

He thought all those thoughts as he went up the stairs. There would have been time to live through a whole life while he climbed. He put his hand on the round curve of the plaster, as he always did. Its little prickling points were invisible to the eye, but he felt them. The door to the room was open and the room was full of sun. Fear prickled him, like the plaster. People had said Nancy would never stand the life, but she had stood it. She was everything he was not, light and graceful, laughing out of a crowd. She would stand with her sisters at the street corner, her skirts blowing, her face whipped with laughter. No one else could dream of belonging in that tight circle.

He loved to watch her. He would rather watch Nancy dancing than dance himself. He would sit very upright, his eyes sharp and distant, his body planted in the chair so that little by little the room felt its presence, and the girls would glance at him as they went by.

They said she would never stand the loneliness of the life, with him gone for his twenty-eight days' duty six times a year. He had moved her ten miles down the coast from her sisters. She'd slept with them every night of her life, she told him. Nancy and Liza together, Hester in the truckle, then Sarey in her cot-bed behind the door. She'd stared round their bedroom the first night they were married, and then she'd taken a run and a jump and landed in the middle of their big bed and let herself fall back with her arms wide, feeling all that space, laughing.

The bed was too big when she lay alone in it. He was an offshore lighthouseman, and she knew that when she married him. If the lighthouse tender couldn't land to change crew on relief day, Nancy might be waiting for him another week. Often the weather was bad when it came to changeover. He'd watch the wall of white foam crash against the glass and know he wasn't going to get off. But Nancy stood it. She had her little garden. She didn't flinch. She knew all the fishing boats and would stand to watch them go out around the point, her skirts blown back against her legs, moulded to them by the wind. He was glad there was no one else to see her like that. She fed her garden with fish-meal and rotted down sea-weed, and when salt storms burnt off the leaves of her spinach and lettuces, she planted again. He would see her kneeling on the path, skirts bunched under her, tamping the seedlings in with her quick fingers.

Sometimes she would walk the ten miles to Carrack Cross to see her sisters, but she would never stay more than one night. When he asked her why she shrugged and said, 'This is my life now.' He would watch her scrambling over the black, sharp rocks, picking mussels at low tide with her skirts kilted up. If she climbed the cliff he knew she could look westward as far as the grey tumble of houses that was Carrack Cross. When she set off with her basket to pick blackberries or early mushrooms, he had to fight the fear that she would never come home again, and that the prints of her stout black boots on the wet fields would be the last thing he would ever see of her.

Slowly, methodically, he would climb the lighthouse tower, towards the light, thinking of her. A mound of sea thudded against the tower, then fell back and weaselled at the foot of the rock, getting its strength. Nancy said she did not mind thinking of him in the lighthouse, no matter how bad the storms, but what she kept out of her thoughts was the moment when he was brought off the landing-platform, with the sea hungry for him and the lighthouse-tender pitching. Sometimes the sight of it came into her mind at night, before she could push it away. It made her sick to think of it, she said, though he knew she could walk to the edge of the cliff and stand there without a moment's dizziness.

He was standing still, not on the steps of the lighthouse tower, but on his own staircase, at home, one hand on the plaster wall. He must go on up to her, where she was waiting for him.

She was there, as he'd known she would be. Her toes pointed up through the sheets and she looked like a child waiting to be kissed goodnight. They'd often thought of when Michael would be old enough to talk to them and have a story at bedtime. Would they teach him to say his night prayers? Nancy thought yes, Blaise no. He knew she already said a prayer over Michael when she put him in his cot. He had no faith in it himself, but believed there was no harm, if Nancy did it.

He stood in the doorway and stared at her toes,

because he was afraid to follow the white sweep of her body up to her face. He had seen terrible things done to the faces of the dead, when the sea got them. Nothing must touch her eyebrows that flexed like two fine black wings when she laughed. Nothing must touch her mouth. He'd noticed her mouth before he noticed anything else about her.

The sunlight was strong. It made him blink. But those windows were dirty. It made you realise what had been blowing onto them all winter. All that salt. It had made a crust on the panes. He would clean them for her. She'd lain there and listened to the rain, all night long sometimes. She never told him that she lay awake, but he knew it from the way the skin under her eyes was dry and sunk with sleeplessness. It had been a dark, long winter, but now it was over.

'Winter's over.' She'd said that yesterday, hearing a scuffle of starlings in the roof-space. He'd wondered if he should smoke out the birds for her. Starlings were filthy things, full of mites. And then she'd said the sun was reaching higher on the wall opposite her bed.

'Look, it's up to that mark on the plaster now.'

She'd pointed. This was a world of her own, in this room. The rest had shrunk away from her, and she no longer asked about it, or even noticed the wood anemones and celandines her sisters brought her, their stems packed into wet moss. The baby sounded far off, though he was only downstairs. These past two weeks she'd stopped asking for Michael. She couldn't hold him any more. Michael was too strong for her. He kicked, and she cried out. It was just weakness, she said, her lips white.

He'd unlaced his boots at the top of the stairs, ready. Now he took them off so there'd be no noise to trouble her. He went over to Nancy and touched her feet. The darn on the counterpane ran up the side of the little tent her body made. She had darned that darn. It was her own fine stitching. He might have watched her do it, but when? Suddenly he saw her, sitting opposite him through the evenings of his off-duty, her polished head moving just a little with each stab of her needle. She didn't look up. Didn't look at him. He had his hand round her feet, holding them tight. Why hadn't they flopped to one side as they did when she relaxed into sleep? When she was deep into her sleep she seemed boneless. She turned away from him, one fist up to her face, dreaming into it.

The bottom stair creaked. Someone coming. There'd been people all the time since they sent Nancy home from the hospital, not able to do any more for her. Her sisters most of all. He put out his hand to fend them off but the next stair creaked, and the next. Someone was walking up, slowly, steadily. As quick as thought he crossed to the door and shut it. There was no bolt, just the latch. No key he could turn. He called out in a voice that was unfamiliar to him.

'Wait. I'll be down.'

There was no answer. Whoever it was stood still, then creaked away, heavily. Maybe it was the doctor. He flushed, alone behind the door, because of his incivility. The doctor was old. He knew Nancy. He didn't whisk in and out, he sat with her. He never left her without making sure that she would be able to hold down the pain until his next visit. You could never pay enough for treatment like that. Blaise would not let her suffer like they'd let her suffer on the ward. He had used up all the money Nancy'd begun to set aside for Michael when she first knew she was pregnant.

All his thoughts turned in him like a cloud of gulls, disturbed. He couldn't bear to let them settle. What if he looked at her again? Which way had they turned her head? Or did it lie as she had turned it?

She was lying with her face toward the window. He almost laughed in relief. After all his thinking, it was easy enough to look at her. What was she doing turned that way, instead of facing the door as she always did when she heard his tread on the stairs? He could see her now, up on her elbows in her white nightgown, with a rosy bruise of sleep on her face where she'd crushed it into the pillow.

But she was turned to the window. Maybe she didn't expect him. She couldn't hear how still the air was, or see how calm the water lay in the bay. In her dreams she thought he was still out at the lighthouse, waiting for the storm to be over so that he could be taken off. When the sea was calm she would always be there to meet him, on the exact day, at the exact hour. She'd have Michael on her hip, shading his eyes against the sun.

A noise burst from his throat. He stumbled back across the floor to her, and knelt at the side of her bed. Her hands were smooth at her sides, outside the bedclothes. Her face was white, but no paler than she'd been many other days. Nancy'd never had much colour even before she was ill. Her hair was a bit untidy on her forehead. So close, he could see tiny grey strands in it. He'd never noticed them before. She was only twenty-nine. In her family they went grey young, but it looked right on them, even youthful. All her sisters had those clear faces and large, beautiful eyes, but he couldn't see the beauty in any of them except her. It was strange to see them in ranks, staring out at you from a photograph. It made Nancy look less herself.

Her eyes were shut. Of course they would be. But he'd seen this closure before. This sunkenness, a gap left by something suddenly gone. Her lids didn't lie lightly over her eyes, cushioned by flowing blood. They seemed to stick to the round globes of her eyeballs. He put out a hand, but against her face it only showed how she had no colour, none at all. He cupped the side of her face. *She's not cold*, he thought triumphantly. Not cold at all. Let them get out of that. He glanced behind him but there was no one there. His breath came lumpily, as if he'd been running. He'd been a good runner, a fine runner once. No use now. She'd seen him pass them all in the men's eight-hundred-yard dash. She'd smiled then. Let them dare say that she was cold.

He felt her again. He snuggled her face against his hand. There was his thumb against her cheek. His thumb looked dirty though he always scrubbed his hands before he came up to her. He was afraid of the way she felt now. Always before when he'd touched her, he'd believed he could feel her blood moving. Her blood ran faster and more brightly than other people's, and closer to the surface of her skin. She had bled a lot when Michael was born. They'd had to throw the mattress away, even though she'd wadded it with newspaper under her. Maybe she was ill then, before they knew it. Nancy might be pale but her fingers were warm in the coldest winter, and she never needed to wear gloves. Sometimes she'd put her hand in his pocket, while they were walking.

Her body lay like a basin of cooling water, neither cold nor hot. He bent over as if to kiss her cheek, but he did not touch her. He was afraid to make a dent in her flesh and see it stay there. Her lips were slightly parted and there was a bubble of saliva on the corner of her mouth. If she'd known it she'd have knocked it away quickly, before he saw it, with the back of her hand.

'Nancy,' he said, quietly, not to embarrass her, the way he'd once pointed out wordlessly that she had a splotch of blood on the back of her pink summer skirt. But she lay still.

From downstairs he heard the noise of a baby crying. Angry, frustrated crying. He listened for a minute before he realised that it was Michael. He'd have been trying to get into the cupboards again. He liked to bang the cups together and smash them. If Nancy'd been downstairs the baby wouldn't have cried. He remembered suddenly how he'd been in the kitchen once when Michael tried to stand against a kitchen chair, then he'd slipped and knocked the corner of his eye as he came down onto the floor. A splash of the baby's blood hit the cardinal red tiles. It was only a little cut but it was deep. Before the baby knew he was hurt Nancy had swooped down and picked him up. In a minute he was smiling, with a clean white handkerchief pressed over his eye. The cut stopped bleeding almost at once, but it left a mark, a thin white line over the eye. That mark was there now.

Downstairs the crying rose to a pitch. The baby would be bucking in the arms of the sister who was holding him, straining his head back and screaming, his face patched red with rage. Then he'd close in and bite, then cry again, frightened at what he'd done. He never used to be like this. Only since Nancy went away to the hospital.

'My wife,' he said aloud, staring at Nancy. It seemed a long time since he had said those words. They were as awkward now as they'd been those weeks after the wedding, when he'd had to shape his lips to it before he could say 'my wife' with an air of ease. And then from one day to the next he'd got used to it, and stopped saying it. He called her Nancy sometimes, but mostly 'you'. He'd said to her this morning, 'Will you be all right? I'm going now, to fetch you the Bengers' Food.'

She needed building up. She could not take solid food, and that was what was weakening her. He had ordered the Bengers' Food for her, and it would be delivered by Trelawny's cart, as far as New Hayle Farm. It was only three miles to walk. He would be back before she knew it.

And she'd said, 'Yes', without smiling, not seeming to pay much attention to him or what was said. He knew she was dull from the stuff the doctor had given her. He hated it, but he knew it was better for her that way. So that was it, he thought now in amazement. That was her last word to me. That flat 'yes', about nothing at all.

The Mixing of Mendhi

Harkiran Dhindsa

Mrs Bancil was watchful. Not that she was likely to meet anyone who might recognise her here, but you never knew. Acquaintances could spring up unexpectedly, like broken paving stones.

She was overwhelmed as printed letters leapt off the glossy covers, merged and melted, blurring indecipherably in front of her.

She tried again to scan the neat rows of magazines, each shiny title elbowing its neighbour for the limelight. Just like she remembered her daughter, Sukhi, in the line of bowing actors in school plays. 'Mummyji, you will take time off work to come and see me, please?' And of course, the mother regularly did, offering up an afternoon of her precious annual leave. Who had known, then, how her child's murmurs would be realised? Mrs Bancil felt a tremulous rush of excitement, followed by . . . by what? Fear? Forced shame?

She was baffled by the vast choice. She'd never known there were so many publications, from those telling readers which car, computer or mobile phone to buy, to those showing people how to groom themselves or their dogs. She averted her eyes quickly from the top shelf, trying to focus on the titles in front of her as she adjusted her bifocals. The deep-set dark eyes narrowed under her spectacle frames, recently updated, although still a

The Mixing of Mendhi

decade behind fashion. Darting cautious eyes wrinkled in concentration under the harsh fluorescent lights of the shop as she tried to read the words.

The language itself was not a problem these days; in fact her English had improved enormously since the death of her husband nine years ago. Whilst *sirdarji* was alive she had relied heavily on him, but now she could fill out forms, pay bills and make enquiries even when she got those exasperating eternal automated touch phone responses. She still called him *sirdarji*, the respectful Punjabi term, whispered it in her head when she thought about him, lamentingly spoke it aloud with accompanying grievous shaking of head if she was talking about him to another. Never, not once, had she called him by his name. Now, and this surprised her more than it did anybody else, even without *sirdarji* she could get on with day-to-day living on her own, including following the soaps on television. He loathed those programmes.

Sometimes she shocked herself when she thought of how she had emerged over the last few years. Not bad, she reckoned for a woman who had come to England at the age of twenty-one with little education and spent the next sixteen years living in the shadow of her austere husband. He would have sneered at the soaps. 'Artificial drama, waste of time watching this rubbish,' he'd have muttered, turning the channel over to the news. Rarely these days did she have to seek her now grown-up daughter's help.

Now what was the name of this magazine? Sukhi had phoned her only yesterday to tell her about it. She tried hard to recall the title, a short word. However, words got lost lately, in some memory myopia. But faltering as she thought her mind was, she had come to know that she could still learn more. It had been a slow realisation, like a late dawn in winter with muted sunlight creeping up inconspicuously. Maybe she could start one of those beginners' computer courses, like Beryl at work was doing. 'That's what'll run everything next century,' Beryl had said at lunch break, painting candy-pink lipstick on to her gradually disappearing lips. 'If you can't work a computer, you'll be left behind. It'll be the new them and us, those who are computer literate and those who aren't.' A few years ago, before she had started evening classes, Beryl would never have used a word like 'literate' and Mrs Bancil wouldn't have understood it.

Determinedly Mrs Bancil searched the display until suddenly, a little louder pattering of her ageing Indian heart, her own eyes met a familiar pair smiling out at her from a magazine cover. Shades of soft browns and watery greens fused together to unfathomable depths in the eyes of her daughter. Here was the face of that beautiful daughter adorning the cover page. She was startled by someone she knew so well displayed in this public territory. But then how much did she know of her at all? How much easier was it not to know, not to ask questions? Just as it was simpler not to have the questions asked by other people – prodding enquiries like 'So, *bhanji*, does your daughter live on her own?'

She stared again at the enigmatic eyes, a mesmerising blend of her own father's pale brown and her husband's hazel. 'Kashmiri eyes,' that's what Mrs Bancil's mother called them. They were like the paler eyes sometimes found amongst the dwellers in the cool mountain ranges of North India, their colour a rarity amongst her own people in the Punjab.

The gleeful grin of a life-size cardboard Santa hauling a sack of books over his shoulder loomed behind Mrs Bancil as she furtively seized a copy of the magazine. Nobody she knew was lurking in the aisles – that's why

The Mixing of Mendhi

she had taken the bus this morning into the town's shopping centre. She could have bought the same magazine in the corner shop just two minutes' walk from her house, but then she would have had to face the owners, the Kumars. And she really had not wanted to engage in a conversation about her daughter with some disapproving busybody. By the afternoon Mrs Kumar would have told all her customers that Mrs Bancil had been in unashamedly buying a magazine that contained pictures of her dissolute daughter.

She scuttled to the counter through the midweek splattering of Christmas shoppers. She excused her journey out by telling herself that she needed a new cardigan and they had a big Marks and Spencer store here in the centre. At the till Mrs Bancil searched for her money in her battered brown leather handbag that always bulged with keys, coins, squashed bundles of tissues in an assortment of pastel shades, and old lottery tickets that she had never got round to checking against the winning numbers. She was aware that it probably seemed incongruous, her a middle-aged Asian woman clutching a magazine ostensibly aimed at young men. She startled the woman behind the counter out of her trance by commenting self-consciously, 'It's for my son.' The sales assistant looked at her quizzically, wondering if she'd missed the beginning of a conversation, and then with a 'just humour the strange' and a retail policy ersatz smile, she said, 'There's two pounds eighty change.'

Mrs Bancil did not actually have any sons, she had only ever given birth to a daughter, Sukhi – a fact that was always a bitter disappointment to her husband, as if he had been shortchanged, as if he was paying the mortgage on a life that he would never be able to fully live out. 'I have noticed,' he once said to his wife in solemn tones, stroking his beard into a wispy point at the centre of his chin, as he was in the habit of doing whenever he was about to sermonise on what he believed to be his own profound gem of wisdom, 'I have noticed that men who only have sons are more light-hearted, they have less to worry about. I have seen them at work, they laugh more, crack jokes.' Sukhi had been standing there in the same room – had heard those words – words that settled on people like dust, got into their lungs, so they choked forever more, like an asthmatic.

Mrs Bancil had wanted to say at the time, that the reason he did not laugh, did not dance along merrily in his life, was not because he lacked a son, but simply because he lacked a sense of humour. But she hadn't said it, instead just nodded her head. Maybe she hadn't even thought to disagree at the time, maybe it was something she was capable of thinking only now.

She often wondered whether, if she had produced a son, this might have softened his stern temperament. Nothing had prepared her for his uncommunicative nature. Her own father had been a gentle, caring man who had outwardly shown as much love to his four daughters as he did to his sons. She remembered his quiet tears as he embraced her at the airport in Delhi one distant dry May, as she was about to leave for England with her present of a pure wool winter coat, hand-made by a reputable tailor her father knew, slung over her arm. 'You'll need it against the cold out there,' he had said.

But good fortune was always balanced by a bad blow, Mrs Bancil believed – a quirk of *kismet* to stop you becoming too complacent, too smug. One reason why she never really wanted to win the lottery jackpot anyway. So it did not surprise her completely then, when she reflected years later, that the man who had been fatefully chosen to be her husband came from a family

The Mixing of Mendhi

that elevated sons to a far higher status than daughters. He considered daughters a liability, especially his own. He saw Sukhi grow. When people remarked, 'She's getting very tall,' Mrs Bancil had said to him, 'You can't stop children growing,' sensing his fear, although it could have been mistaken for disgust. It should have been pride that he felt, as Sukhi emerged into the beautiful teenager with those entrancing hazel eyes, but her latent sexuality was repugnant to him. 'Tell her not to wear skirts, she should wear salwar kameez at home.' And he tightened the reins. Outside was another world: depraved, debauched, where you couldn't trust a daughter and even less could you trust the world with a beautiful one. You read all sorts of prurient stories in the local Indian newspaper, too.

Sukhi, however, wanted to be an actress. A profession that Mr Bancil considered to be on a plane not much higher than a prostitute. 'I've been at the maths club,' Sukhi usually said on her days late home from school. Mrs Bancil knew very well that Sukhi was rehearsing for the school play, but would make no comment. She did not want to appear to be condoning her daughter's activities. After all, she knew it was always mothers who were blamed for not keeping a strict enough hold on their daughters. She did not want to reprimand the girl either; back in India she and her sisters had often sat totally submerged in the glorious glamour of the musicals shown in the cinema houses, so captivated that once the flickering reel had begun to roll they became oblivious to the stifling heat, suspended in the sweat that rose off the packed audience around them.

Sukhi's English teacher had said that she had a genuine talent for acting. Her father had been perturbed by this comment at the parents' evening and had suggested that she concentrate on her maths instead. Then, when Sukhi was only sixteen years old, her father had died of a heart attack, suddenly. And whilst Mrs Bancil continued mourning, Sukhi, well, Sukhi was just growing, catching up on growing completely as only the unfettered can. Being a widow gave Mrs Bancil an excuse for letting Sukhi just be. '*Bhanji*,' she said to the neighbourhood women, 'it is difficult, you know, on my own.' Quickly she discovered the effectiveness of this pathos.

It was fine now on her own, she thought, as she watched the scurrying shoppers through the steamed-up windows of the bus. The Christmas lights would be switched on soon, and in place of the perennial Christmas message swung across the front of the precinct, spelled in a chain of white light bulbs was 'Happy Millennium'. She knew what *sirdarji* would have said in his cynicism – 'Another excuse for commercialism, nobody's going to wake up feeling any better just because it's another New Year's Day.' She still missed him sometimes, in spite of himself, in spite of herself. After all, in the end he cared, worked hard to pay for their comfort, exhausting himself at the electronics factory through the night shift, a work schedule that inadvertently gave Sukhi the chance to watch all the forbidden late-night films on television. He had cared overwhelmingly, restrictively.

Reaching home, Mrs Bancil hurriedly pulled the magazine from her bag. Her impatience to see the article was so great that she spared her usual ritual of making a cup of tea first. Without removing her coat, she flicked through the pages. Another photograph of her daughter, her face cupped in her hands, this time a stillness in the eyes whose more usual fluidity was capable of revealing and hiding so many thoughts. Something of her father in that expression, thought Mrs Bancil. She fingered the

The Mixing of Mendhi

glossy picture, her own daughter a professional actress, her dream realised at last. 'Eastern Promise' was written under the photograph. Mrs Bancil laughed; Sukhi had only once been to India. She started to read what it said about the actress, about this not quite unknown stranger. This was her own girl who used to step out from behind the red velvet curtains in the front room and take a bow, saying 'Thank you, ladies and gentlemen.'

Mrs Bancil did not comprehend every word of the review but she understood that it was praising the new film for its originality and applauding her daughter's acting. She had not seen the film yet. Sukhi had invited her to the première, adding 'You might find some of it a bit uncomfortable to watch, there's a scene in which I have to take my clothes off.' It had been difficult for the daughter to admit that, Mrs Bancil knew.

'Oh dear, couldn't you act in something where you didn't have to do that sort of thing?' It was just as difficult for the mother to respond.

'Mummyji, it's the first really good role I've been offered. It's not just a stereotype, or just a bit part. This is what I've been waiting for.'

So Mrs Bancil saved herself and her daughter the embarrassment by declining to go to the première. Images of bare skin entered her mind and were not quite dismissed – the softness of a child bathed in water, in a room being kept warm by a bar heater, before they had central heating; the potential of skin as the child tells you she has just started her periods and hushed explanations, knowing your daughter already knew more than you did. She would wait till they released the film on video.

Mrs Bancil closed the magazine. She got up to make that cup of tea, the way she liked it, letting the water boil up with the tea leaves, milk and sugar in the pan, adding a cardamom to give that thick Indian brew. A magpie swooped down and strutted around in a cocksure manner, pecking at the bread she had left out on the frosted grass in the garden. You hardly ever saw sparrows these days. Funny that, because she remembered how years ago, there were so many sparrows flitting around the London gardens. So similar to the ones in India, they had become her favourite bird. But in those days, you didn't see crows in this neighbourhood, like the one now cawing amongst the denuded branches of the apple tree. In India these birds were bold, hurtling in and scooping pieces of chapatti out of the hands of small children. She remembered a particularly menacing crow leaving her younger brother crying on the veranda once when he was a toddler. The same brother who, a few years later, in some unintentional revenge on the bird world, crouched down behind the hibiscus bushes, waiting to pounce on a sparrow. He and his scrawny cousin dipped the sparrow in blue dye before releasing the hapless bird to hop around under the weight of its congealed feathers. The plan for these experimenting village ragamuffins was to see if they might catch the marked sparrow again another day. Mrs Bancil recalled the blood-red brightness of the hibiscus flowers, static observers in the still air.

Strange, though, the things you did see in London these days, little associations of India, like crows and *dahl* and *roti* in Tescos and *mendhi* on the hands of white girls. And *sirdarji* had been afraid of losing it all. But then he would still have muttered rancorous words against this adoption of fragments of Indian culture. His boundaries had been clear, none of this blurring of the edges and gradually losing the ground you stood upon. 'We have to preserve what we are, remember where we came from. If they start drinking now, then they will be losing all their inhibitions and be wanting to wear

The Mixing of Mendhi

bikinis,' he had once said in one of his leaps of logic when Mrs Bancil had told him that sherry had been offered at the work Christmas lunch and some of the Indian women had accepted a glass. The fact that his wife spent her days packing up heavy bottles of gin at the local factory was fine, as long as the alcohol only passed through her hands.

When they went on their visit back to India, they never mentioned the alcohol. 'It's a bottling plant,' they had said, 'you know, soft drinks.' Well, no need to reveal all. After all, her sister-in-law worked in a factory where on the wall lights perpetually lit up orange bubbles being poured into a glass. An eternal stream, trickling away, the way Mrs Bancil had always remembered it from her thousands of bus journeys up and down the Great West Road. A stalwart amongst all the new light industry springing up, amongst the shining glass and chrome buildings that postured like suited-up young men, confident in their newness.

Along that perpetually evolving highway of manufacturing, she and the other Indian ladies could still be seen queuing daily at the bus stop in their headscarves and winter coats over their salwar kameezes. They'd just got greyer or stopped dying their hair, now that they were grandmothers. They still talked about what they were going to cook tonight, only these days it was Mrs Chopra saying how wonderful her daughter-in-law was and always had the chapattis made by the time she got home, and Mrs Grewel retorting how did she have the luck to get one like that, all hers was interested in was sitting down in front of *EastEnders*. Some things changed so quickly and others, well, they just trailed along, occasionally nudged by the currents around them. Ebbs and flows. You forgot and expected places to be as you had left them, locked away in some time vault of your own memory. Instead there was her last trip to Delhi, where perhaps she shouldn't have been startled by the pizza and burger chain restaurants springing up amongst the ramshackle sticky tea stalls. And maybe she ought not to have been surprised by the jarring image of the group of young women with loose hair flicking around their bare brown arms, chatting gaily, assuredly with a record stall vendor, whilst a bullock took a dump in the middle of the seething street.

The cardamom shell bobbed on the bubbles of the tea like a drowning insect. Mrs Bancil turned down the flame. She could spend time on the garden now that she was retiring from the spirits factory. There would be no blood-red hibiscus, but she could start by clearing some of the weeds, maybe encouraging a few more sparrows. Beryl had said you could attract them by putting up the right sort of seed dispenser.

She looked through the beaded partition at the faded curtains that still hung in the room, now a little frayed. She must replace them, she could use the money that Sukhi had sent her last month. She hadn't wanted to take money from her daughter, but Sukhi had insisted, saying, 'Thank you for putting up with me.' She stared back at the face of her beautiful daughter on the magazine cover. 'Secret of Sukhi's Success' was emblazoned under the magazine title. So, in some people's eyes her daughter is a success. *Sirdarji's* failure. She wondered if she would ever see intricate *mendhi* patterns painted on the hands of her daughter, with the sweet tangy smell of the freshly mixed green paste, so evocative of prenuptial preparations and bashful brides of old.

The family in the house opposite had turned on their Christmas lights. There would be no bustling holiday family gathering for her. She would sit alone in the room, faded like the old curtains. Maybe she'd watch the Christmas programmes, the Queen's speech. *Sirdarji* always watched that. Sukhi hadn't said what she was up to, busy probably with her friends.

On the way home from the bus, Mrs Bancil had seen that they were showing her daughter's film at the local independent cinema. Yes, there was much that could be done, much to be planned in retirement and tomorrow, well, tomorrow she could go to see the film. She hadn't stepped inside a cinema for years, not since the Liberty building in Southall was still showing films, before the advent of videos had turned it into a market, before it burnt down. An Indian woman going to the cinema on her own, what would they say, what would he have said, and if she bumped into Mrs Kumar, well, maybe this time she would just tell the truth.

Reshape Whilst Damp

Ros Barber

When I was six, I thought being a mermaid was a career choice. I had seen one in the swimming pool at Clacton Butlins, where you could watch people underwater through the reinforced glass as you gulped down a Knickerbocker Glory. Until that first half-term trip to Butlins, I had thought that Knickerbocker Glories were a figment of Paddington Bear's imagination, and was beginning to doubt that mermaids were any more real. But there I was, with all the components of a Knickerbocker Glory sliding down my throat and an underwater view of swimmers that I had only previously seen done in the Clacton Dolphinarium, when I saw a flash of tail and scale and fin, a hairless torso attached. She smiled at me, and I smiled back, and for three or four minutes she stayed there, her hair Medusan water snakes, and not a bubble escaping her lips. There was only me and her, you understand; Mum had taken little sister to the toilet and Dad was disputing the bill with the counter staff. No one else was in the café; and no wonder, Dad said later, because it was so bloody overpriced.

'Hey Chloe!' Dad said. 'Bring that ice-cream back up here!'

I glanced at him urgently, said, 'Dad, look, look!'

But when I turned back there were just some legs

half-dissolved in the distance, and flowery one-pieces, and black knee-length trunks.

Uncle Gerald and Auntie Irene came to visit at Easter. They said, as grown-ups always did, how much we'd grown. (Adults always say this as if they are amazed; it is simply that by growing, children can do the one thing that they no longer can; adults are better at everything else, but are not so good at growing.) After the most popular comment of infrequently-visiting relations, they asked the most common question: what were we going to be when we grew up? (That growing thing again, in other words, when you've stopped doing the thing you currently do best, you'll have to choose something else to be good at, and we want to know what that thing will be.) Naturally, our answers would change from year to year, even from week to week, and on this occasion my sister said, 'I want to work in Woolworth's,' because she had been there that day and was overawed by the range of pocketable delights on the button counter.

'What about you, Chloe?'

'I want to be a mermaid.'

And that seemed to please them; I remember they laughed and Dad tousled my top-knot, and so it was decided. A mermaid I would be.

My ambition became a family joke. People were comfortable with it. 'Chloe wants to be a mermaid.' It never failed to cheer up my parents. On beach holidays at Porthcurno, Swanage, Bideford, I would wrap a swathe of green and silver lurex around my middle (Mum was kind enough to provide this; it went into the boot with the wind-break and castle-shaped buckets), and lounge mermaid-like on the dunes. When it was breezy, Dad would exhort me to wear a T-shirt, but I always replied that mermaids didn't shop at Marks and

Spencers. Mum would laugh and tell him to humour me, and then he'd laugh too. For a few years I thought they had it the wrong round – wasn't I 'humouring' them?

Then, suddenly, they ceased to find it funny. I can pin down this moment to a shopping trip a few days after my thirteenth birthday; Mum said she was buying me a 'training' bra. When I asked the assistant what this uncomfortable contraption was supposed to be 'training' me for, she blushed and replied, 'Growing breasts, dear.'

'Oh,' I said, disappointed.

'What did you think it was training you for?' she said.

This was the point at which Mum would usually chip in helpfully, 'She wants to be a mermaid', but she was silent and flushed. So I said it for her. The assistant stopped fiddling with the shoulder straps and looked me full in the face.

'What do you mean, dear?'

'You know, a mermaid, like Marina in *Stingray*.'

'But she's a puppet.'

'So's Troy, but isn't he a dish?' I said. Mum was completely failing to come to my assistance, for some reason.

'But *he's* a puppet.'

'What, I can't fancy a puppet? What about Virgil Tracy in *Thunderbirds*, he's gorgeous.'

'Don't be silly,' Mum said sharply.

That sudden about-face. For years and years it was all right to fancy puppets and want to be a mermaid, and the next week, it wasn't. I mean, I wasn't stupid. I knew damn well that puppets were puppets and people were people. Was that going to stop me fancying Troy and Virgil? Of course not. They were a darn sight more interesting (and less spotty) than Paul Whittock and Dean Saunders, the only human offerings at school. And just because Marina was a puppet mermaid, it didn't mean mermaids didn't exist, any more than Troy being a puppet meant humans didn't exist.

'Mermaids don't exist,' Mum said as she whisked me down the High Street with the other hand clenched on the carrier bag. I appealed to Dad when we got home and he simply said I wasn't going to be lounging around on any beaches half-naked anymore. He revealed he had already thrown out my strip of green lurex. Well, I knew to keep quiet after that, but it occurred to me that parents were as stupid as they were fickle. Dumping the lurex wasn't going to stop me being a mermaid.

They seemed pleased when I threw myself into swimming lessons. They didn't see the link, even though Dad often said to us how effort and achievement went hand in hand. They applauded me for racing through the badges (including survival bronze, silver and gold). It seemed clear to me that once all the possible badges were sewn onto my towel (expertly by my mother, at first, then at her insistence, by myself in ungainly, crab claw stitches), I would automatically begin to sprout the required scales and fins, and have no need for a new strip of lurex. But all that happened was that I was invited to join the junior swimming club at the sports centre.

I scoured the local library for information: stories and sightings and famous fakes. The repeated assertion (which grew no more plausible on repetition) that mermaids are sea-cows as viewed through the eyes of inebriated sailors. As if even cheap rum could make a person mistake those dog-faced dugongs for beautiful scale-tailed women. But none of these books offered a way into my calling. I was at a loss.

Then, just after my fifteenth birthday, the careers guidance lady arrived at our school with forms that they could run through their (newly acquired) computer system, aptly named CASCADE (I could almost hear the water running over my body, the bubbles and foam). Of course, the career would choose *you* rather than the other way round, but I was certain that from the boxes I checked (Was I a people person? No. Did I like animals? Yes. Did I like making things? No) and the useful supplementary information I gave (Hobbies: swimming – competitive and for pleasure, favourite location: seaside) that a letter would come back pressing me to enrol as a mermaid as soon as possible.

When the results arrived, I was saddened to find that the career that had chosen me was veterinary assistant – not even a full-blown vet, because you'd have to be a people-person for that – but such, I reasoned, were the limitations of computers. Marine biologist was a secondary option, but I'd need a good degree for that and there was a sub-clause that said, in a roundabout way, I wasn't bright enough.

The careers guidance lady came back to discuss the results with us. We had ten-minute interview slots.

'And you are – Chloe. What did you think about the results, Chloe?'

I told her they were very disappointing.

'Well, we're still testing the computer system. This is the first year we've used it, so your feedback would be helpful. How were they disappointing?'

Now, as I've said before, I wasn't stupid. I had worked out I shouldn't go around talking about mermaids. Not like Philip Angmering who just went on and on about double-decker buses and brought one into every story he wrote, every picture he painted, every chemistry experiment he wrote up. I didn't want to end up wasting each Wednesday after school with a child psychologist when it would mean less time to practise my underwater lengths (I was building up lung capacity; not for me the crafty ten-pack of Rothmans in the Co-op car park). So I told her I just didn't see myself as a veterinary assistant, and that I would wait to see what exam results I got. She was more interested in assessing the computer system than finding me a vocation in any case, so after a brief grilling (never comfortable for one who thinks of herself as half-fish) she let me off the hook.

I decided my best hope was working at the Clacton Dolphinarium, but two weeks before I left school the Council closed it down because the dolphins kept dying. And so I found myself selling fish – live ones, not the battered and breadcrumbed variety – at the tropical fish shop that occupied a corner of the Garden Centre. Netting them gently for impulse buyers or regulars ('She'll never get on with your Kissing Gourami, Mr Tate; how about one of these Black Mollies instead?'), I was anxious, sending up prayers to protect them from white spot and fin rot, reminding the customer about the importance of regularly checking the water acidity. My welling eyes sold armfuls of pH testing kits; gallons of 'TapSafe'; my boss considered me an excellent employee, if a little weird. And when it was quiet and the stocktaking done, I wandered around the glowing tanks in the dark, admiring the overlap of scale, the infinite variety of fin, and above all, the absence of surfacing – the slow beat of gill. I ran a hand wistfully under my jawbone.

'Steve here?' said a voice. The Garden Centre manager.

'No,' I replied.

'You'll do.'

And our eyes solidified.

So I married a dry man; a man who enjoyed getting his

hands dirty. A man who sold compost, chipped bark, 'fish-blood-'n'-bone'. My parents liked him all the more for bringing me down to earth.

'Got his feet on the ground,' Dad said approvingly. 'Just what you need.'

He got a promotion within the chain and we moved to Banbury. A place that boasted, as several English towns do, to be the most central (sea-distant) spot in the British Isles.

A fish out of water. I couldn't find another job there, so I got pregnant. From the moment the waters broke and that first crumpled head emerged, my life became blissfully wet once more. I enjoyed it: bathing the baby, washing her cardigans by hand, taking her swimming as soon as she'd had her jabs. They say if you catch babies early enough they still have the reflex to hold their breath, remembered from the womb. By six months she could swim out of her depth; smiling at me under water, her eyes gleaming like marbles.

For the next one, I chose a water birth. We rented a big tub and filled it up with a hose and steaming kettles. I was huge the second time – a whale calving – but I was beginning to feel like a mermaid again. On the second canister of gas-and-air, I was so out of myself I was convinced I could see scales on my shins.

Unfortunately for my husband, my conviction persisted into the following weeks. Our GP diagnosed postnatal depression. I was admitted to a mother and baby unit for women with 'my problem'. Except the others didn't have 'my problem'. They weren't crying just for the feeling of salt-water on their skin. And they didn't have an instruction on their notes that they weren't allowed to have unsupervised baths because of their penchant for trying to drown themselves. I tried to explain that I wasn't drowning myself; I was simply extending my ability to hold my breath underwater. The staff didn't believe that five minutes thirty seconds was even possible. They put me on anti-psychotics. Nine weeks of my life were washed completely blank. My psychiatrist kept hinting I had been sexually abused as a child, and was in denial. The nurses told me my 'scales' were really eczema. Once I had grasped this, I was shipped home with my squalling son and a prescription for anti-depressants.

Of course, I took him swimming, and he launched himself into the chlorinated blue even faster than his sister. I knew he was born to it.

My eczema didn't get any better. Patches appeared on my knees, my hips, my waist. The GP said it was stress and gave me a cream to rub in. The redness went away, and the patches turned a silvery-green. In the middle of the night, sleepless beside my slumbering husband, I picked at them. They bled through my jeans when I hoovered the stairs; an almost ecstatic pain. The GP said I now had *infected* eczema and instructed the practice nurse to dress the patches regularly. He said I should avoid both swimming and bathing, but instead, sponge around the bandages.

It was about this time that my husband said he was leaving me. He said that I physically revolted him, that he couldn't bear to touch me. He said I had changed, that I wasn't the woman he'd married. He moved in with his personal assistant. I cried for a few days, and felt a lot better for it.

I think houses sense when the practical partner has left, because within weeks it was falling apart. The guttering came away in a heavy rainstorm. Pipes started to burst, and everywhere I looked there were puddles. Most mornings I had to carry the children, one by one, across the flooded kitchen to the breakfast table. The health visitor was horrified and said I should get a plumber in immediately or she would have to call Social Services. I picked up the Yellow Pages and rang a number from the line ads. In the late evening, I answered the door.

'Darius,' he said. 'You have a leak?'

He shook the water off his boots and stepped from the rain into my wetlands.

'You have a *leak*,' he said, gazing around awestruck.

'I have lots of leaks, I think,' I replied. 'I can't even work out where it's coming from.'

'Is the power still on?'

I followed his eyes to a power point that was barely above the water line.

'I'll get it off *now*,' he said, a little white. 'And where's your stop-cock?'

I didn't know.

'Don't worry,' he said, 'I'll find it.' And waded past me, his toolbox rattling.

I read a story to Elise, feeding Samuel at the breast as I did so, and put them both to bed. Downstairs was nothing but the serenity of water. I couldn't hear the tapping of pipes, the hush of a blowtorch or other plumber-y noises. Just a plip now and then, but mostly that solid, embracing silence that still water exudes. The silence so intense that I could have believed we were all twenty fathoms down on the ocean floor.

The bottom of the stairs had vanished. How the water could have risen so quickly I didn't know, but it was waist-high as I waded to the kitchen. And there he was, face down, unconscious. Floating.

Still.

I rushed forwards and rolled him over like a log; his lips blue-tinged, his skin pale.

'Mister Darius!' I croaked. I tried to remember how

to do the kiss of life. I had no idea; I'd only seen it on films. As I brought my lips to his, his eyelids fluttered.

'Jesus! I thought you were dead!'

'No, no,' he said, struggling to his feet. 'Must have knocked myself out. I tripped over something. He reached down shoulder-deep and brought up a saucepan.

'I'm sorry,' I said, 'Elise must have taken it out of the cupboard to play with.'

'That's okay,' he replied. 'Water's lovely stuff, but dangerous around the house. Best in the open. I love the ocean.'

'Oh, so do I!' I blurted, embarrassing myself.

The water around him was turning a faint red.

'You've cut yourself,' I said, mortified.

'I'm fine.'

'No, let me take a look. Hop up on the table.'

His trousers were gashed; the skin gashed beneath them. I found a dry tea-towel and mopped the wound.

'Let me wrap something around it,' I said. 'I have steri-strips, but I think you might need stitches. It's quite—'

I peered more closely. Now that the blood flow was stemmed, I noticed the surrounding skin: scaly. Like mine.

'—deep.'

We stared at each other.

'You have eczema too,' I said.

'Eczema?' he smiled.

'Like me,' I said, pulling down my waistband to show him an inch of hip.

What happened then was a bit surprising. He jumped off the table. And I found myself, waist-high in water, snogging the plumber. We were mingling tongues; I was drinking from his mouth. He unzipped himself, let his trousers fall into the water.

Scales: green-blue-and-silver scales, diamond-shaped, overlapping. Fish scales. Merman scales. I ran my hands over them, amazed.

'You too,' he said. 'You too.' And gripped me as I rolled my leggings down. He peeled off the bandages. 'Look,' he said. 'Look!'

Afterwards, we dressed ourselves and loaded the sleeping children into his car.

'They can swim?' he whispered as he pulled my seat-belt into position.

'Like fish,' I said.

He smiled and started the engine.

'Where do you want to go from?'

'Swanage,' I said. 'Definitely Swanage.'

About the Authors

Ros Barber was born in 1964 in Washington D.C. She works as a part-time creative writing tutor for the University of Sussex. Her poetry has been commended in the Arvon and National Poetry competitions, anthologised by Faber, and appears in Virago's 1999 *Writing Women*. Her short fiction has been published by Bloomsbury, and she was a prize-winner in the *Independent on Sunday*/Bloomsbury Short Story Competition 1997. She lives in Hove, Sussex.

Elspeth Barker was born and educated in Scotland and Oxford. Her first novel *O Caledonia* was published in 1992 and her second comes out this year. As a journalist and book reviewer she has written extensively for magazines and newspapers.

Clare Bayley was awarded an MA in Playwriting from Birmingham University in 1993. She won the 1996 Times Screenwriting Award, and the resulting screenplay, *Corridors in the Air*, is currently being developed with Zephyr Films. She wrote the script for *The Shift*, a collaborative play directed by Andy Lavender and performed by the Young Vic Studio in 1997. Her stage play, *Northern Lights*, was performed at the Grove Theatre, London in 1994 and subsequently adapted for the Saturday Play on BBC Radio 4 in 1996. *Blavatsky*, another collaboration with Andy Lavender, was performed at the Young Vic Studio in 1999. She is also a journalist and former Theatre Editor of the *Independent*.

Helen Cleary was born in Chester in 1971. She currently

About the Authors

lives in Norfolk working as a freelance editor and writer and attending the creative writing MA at the University of East Anglia.

Harkiran Dhindsa was born in Punjab, India in 1964. She came to England at the age of three and grew up in Hounslow. She had a traditional Punjabi upbringing, juxtaposed with attending an Anglican secondary school. She qualified as a dentist in 1988 from King's College, London and now works as a community dentist. She is married with two sons, and lives in Barnet, Herts.

Helen Dunmore is a poet, novelist and short-story writer. Her novel, *A Spell of Winter*, won the first Orange Prize in 1996. Her most recent novel is *With Your Crooked Heart*, and her latest collection of short stories is *Ice Cream*.

Vicky Grut was born in South Africa in 1961 and lived in Madagascar and Italy before moving to England in 1980 to do a Fine Art degree at Goldsmiths' College. Her short stories have been published in magazines and collections since 1994. She has worked in the independent video sector, in adult education, as an academic book editor and for the *New Yorker* magazine in London. She is currently working part-time as an administrator at London's Institute of Contemporary Arts. She has completed her first novel and has begun work on her second. She lives in London with her partner and their eight-year-old son.

Sarah Johnson, a New Zealander who has been living in the UK for the last five years, currently lives in Stirling, where she writes and edits travel and technical books. She has had stories published in various magazines in New Zealand and the UK.

About the Authors

Ann Jolly spent her formative years in Glasgow and now lives near Chichester after two spells in East Africa, working as a court welfare officer and as a private counsellor. She has won several writing competitions, including the Ian St James Awards in 1998 and is now working on a novel based on her experiences in Africa.

Marion Mathieu is a New York-born painter who began writing in 1989. Her pamphlet *Gangster in the Mirror* won the 1995 Jackson's Arm Poetry Pamphlet competition. She was one of the three poets selected for the 1997 New Voices' tour and was awarded a writer's bursary by East Midland Arts. Her short story, 'Facing Charlie', was one of the winners of the 1998 Fish Short Story Prize and appeared in the collection *Scrap Magic*. Four of her poems were included in the 1999 *Writing Women*/Virago anthology *Wild Cards*. She is currently living in Dublin.

Aoi Matsushima was born in 1964 in Tokyo and lived there until 1997 when she gave up her career in PR and advertising to come to Britain to realise her dream of becoming a writer in English. She won the 1998 Ian St James Award for her short story, 'Insurance', and has just completed an MA in Creative Writing at Bath. She lives in London and works as an editor and translator.

Kate Mosse has written two non-fiction books: *Becoming a Mother*, *The House* (which accompanied the award-winning BBC television series on the Royal Opera House, Covent Garden), two novels, *Eskimo Kissing* and *Crucifix Lane*, as well as many short stories and articles. She is the Co-Founder, first Administrator and now the Honorary Director of the Orange Prize for Fiction. Since 1998, she has been Deputy Director of the Chichester Festival Theatre in West Sussex, the first

About the Authors

woman to hold the position. She lives in Bognor Regis with her partner and children.

Michèle Roberts has written eight novels, including *Daughters of the House*, which was shortlisted for the 1992 Booker Prize and won the W H Smith Literary Award. *Impossible Saints* was published in 1997 and *Fair Exchange* in 1999. She lives in London and France.

Ruth Shabi was born in London to an English mother and Iraqi father. She worked in advertising in London before moving to Scotland where she was a member of the Traverse Theatre Writers' group. She moved back to London to work at the BBC and continues to write in her spare time.

Barbara Trapido's first novel *Brother of the More Famous Jack*, won a Whitbread Special Prize for Fiction in 1982 and *Temples of Delight* was shortlisted for the *Sunday Express* Book of the Year in 1990. Her fifth novel, *The Travelling Hornplayer*, was shortlisted for the Whitbread Novel of the Year in 1998. She is currently working on her sixth book.

Lynne Truss is the author of three comic novels and a number of plays and scripts for Radio 4. She is also an award-winning columnist who writes for *The Times*. Her latest book is *Going Loco*.